A Dead

"Who are y

He had already decided how to play it. "I'm an agent. My name is Carter. Nick Carter."

"Israeli?"

"American."

She shrugged. "Same thing."

"Not quite. Being American, I'm slightly more neutral. My arms are starting to hurt like hell."

"Too bad."

"Look, lady, if I wanted you dead, you'd be dead. I want to talk."

"What about?"

"The Jordan Plan, the two missiles, and your insane friends."

NICK CARTER IS IT!

FROM THE NICK CARTER
KILLMASTER SERIES

MIDDLE EAST MASSACRE

KILL MASTER

NICK CARTER

JOVE BOOKS, NEW YORK

KILLMASTER #249: MIDDLE EAST MASSACRE

A Jove Book/published by arrangement with
The Condé Nast Publications, Inc.

PRINTING HISTORY
Jove edition/May 1989

ISBN: 0-515-10014-5

Jove Books are published by The Berkley Publishing Group,
200 Madison Avenue, New York, New York 10016.
The name "JOVE" and the "J" logo
are trademarks belonging to Jove Publications, Inc.

PRINTED IN THE UNITED STATES OF AMERICA

10 9 8 7 6 5 4 3 2 1

Dedicated to the men and women of the
Secret Services of the
United States of America

ONE

The café was off the Avenue de Paris near the port crossing at the Mediterranean Sea. It was less than fifty paces from the imaginary green line that separated the Christian east from the Moslem west in Beirut.

Because of its location, most of the buildings around it had been reduced to rubble during the fighting. Now, with the cease-fire and the Syrians running the country in conjunction with the Lebanese, business had returned to normal.

Still, because it was so close to both sides, the café was an ideal place for a quiet, uninterrupted meeting. The people who passed through its doors knew enough to see nothing and hear less.

At this time of evening, only a quarter of the tables were filled. Two stools were occupied at the bar, one by a scruffy youth in jeans and a dirty shirt. From the lifeless look in his eyes it was obvious that he had been putting a far stronger substance into his body than just beer.

On the other occupied stool sat an attractive woman of about thirty. She had black hair with brown highlights, done in a kind of knot behind her neck. Her brown eyes were wide and, from a distance, looked innocent. Up close they were hard and unblinking. She wore a dark blue blouse and a matching skirt that hugged her hips but flared outward to her knees.

Over the panties beneath the skirt, she wore a garter belt affair that secured a 9mm Beretta automatic between her legs.

When she turned her face to the light, her skin was like delicate Syrian porcelain. But she wasn't Syrian. Her name was Yushi Nuhr. She was Palestinian, and the second in command of the remnant PLO army left in Beirut.

As she sipped a brandy she studied the street through the window and the woman sitting alone at a table in the darker recesses of the café.

Satisfied, she upended her glass and moved to the tiny, dark hallway that led to the rest rooms. A second reason for choosing this particular café was that it had one of the few pay phones in Beirut that worked.

"Rabani, it's me."

"Yes."

"She is here, alone. And I am sure that she was not followed."

"How will I know her?"

"She is very tall, has black hair, and is wearing a black suit with a deep neckline. Right now she is the only other woman besides myself in the bar."

"And police?" the male voice asked.

"None, I am sure of it."

"I will be right there." The line went dead.

Yushi returned to the bar and ordered another brandy. Five minutes later, a dark Renault 12 sedan pulled up across from the café. Two men, both dark with heavy beards, got out of the front and moved into doorways to the front and rear of the car.

Two minutes later, Rabani Saif, the head of the upstart Palestinian splinter group that had refused to leave

Lebanon with Yassir Arafat after the Israeli invasion, got out of the back seat.

Saif was tall and thin, and wore his thick black hair long. He had a full black beard trimmed sketchily into a point at the chin. His eyes were dark and piercing, and they had an expression suggesting he knew something no one else knew. He wore frayed, faded jeans and a blue denim shirt with two top buttons missing.

He glided into the café, looked around, and headed for the bar. He took a stool several spaces away from Yushi with no one between them. About fifty feet behind them, the bartender was serving the other woman a drink.

"How many has she had?" Saif asked, scarcely moving his lips.

"Three."

"Good, that means she is extremely nervous."

When the bartender returned, Saif ordered a Pernod and poured half a glass of water over the yellowish liquid.

"I'm going over. Watch my back."

"Don't I always?" Yushi Nuhr murmured.

Saif moved through the tables and without a word slid into the chair across from the woman.

"I am Rabani Saif." He watched her eyes widen, her body tense, and her hand on the now empty glass tighten. *That's good*, he thought, *she knows the name and fears it*. "You said you had proof that Julian Daoud is a traitor to our cause."

"I feel like a traitor myself," she said. "May I have another drink? I don't usually drink so much, or at least not so quickly. But I need some kind of outside courage, or my own may suddenly run out and I'll never find any more."

Saif signaled the bartender.

When the drink came she sipped instead of gulping it, and Saif found himself drawn to the beauty of her, to the golden lure of her alabaster skin. It occurred to him that that might be precisely what she was . . . a decoy, bait, or a payoff. Her hair was like some impossibly ebony metal burnished until it gleamed at every strand, her mouth was full and rich with promises, and the cameo quality of her face was marked with that trace of sadness that brings determined men to their knees. She could be many things to a man . . . sensuous mistress, enjoyable companion, a wife to make a man hurry home.

But Saif knew differently. She was a traitor. Her name was Marie Boulard, and she was a money-hungry little bitch who was willing to sell her soul, let alone her employer and lover of five years.

"You said you have proof that Daoud the banker is giving all our plans to the other side."

"I do."

"What other side?"

Marie Boulard leaned forward, pulling his eyes down to the shadowed cleft that plunged down, down into her blouse. "The Israelis."

A chill ran up Saif's spine and raised the hairs on the back of his neck. For three years now, since the inception of the Jordan Plan, Julian Daoud had been their money handler. It was Daoud who had laundered their funds and money around the world so the operation would go smoothly. In this position, Daoud had eventually become privy to practically the entire plan.

"You have proof of this?" Saif murmured stonily.

She nodded emphatically. "Proof, and the name of his control. It is a woman, in London. Do you have the money?"

Saif glanced around the room. Not one eye was

looking in their direction. He took an envelope from under his shirt and, shielding it with his body, set it in front of her on the table. "Fifty thousand francs. That is half."

Her white teeth came forward to gnaw on her lower lip. She was selling Julian cheap and she knew it. But she was going mad with fear in Lebanon, and since she had found out the dangerous game her lover was playing, her fear had begun to consume her. She had to get back to Paris.

She reached into her purse and took out an envelope of her own. She hoped he didn't see her hand shaking as she set it on the table and snatched the one with the money.

When her purse clamped shut on the money she could almost see herself walking down the Champs-Elysées. Dear God, she was almost home.

The contents of the second envelope were copies of telexes to the Jarces Bank in Paris. They were a jumble of money transfer requests, itemized bills of lading for collateral, and dates of certain shipments arriving in Lebanon.

To the average reader they would appear as normal, everyday business. But to Rabani Saif, one of the three brains behind the Jordan Plan, they were death. Because he knew the plan, he could see how Daoud had passed it along.

"Son of a bitch," he hissed quietly, then looked back up at the frightened woman. "These were all sent to a bank in Paris. You said his Israeli control was in London."

Marie Boulard leaned forward and pointed a long crimson nail at the destination code at the bottom of each message. It read REBA-ERX.

"ERX means personal, eyes only. The 'eyes only' is

to REBA. There is a special telephone, one with an extension in the bedroom. Julian doesn't like to get out of bed once he is in it. Last night he got a call from London. It was a woman. He told her he would call back." She paused to sip her drink.

Saif drummed his fingers on the table impatiently. "Go on."

"He went into the living room. I counted the clicks as he dialed, and then I listened. He called the woman Reba. She told Julian that the operation would be mounted tonight, so he should make himself invisible for the next seventy-two hours."

"What operation?" Saif hissed.

"I don't know—they didn't say. This morning I called that London number and got a maid. I told her I was the post and there was a problem with the mail. The name is Reba Wallace and the address is Twelve Corning Lane, Belgravia."

Saif listened intently, his eyes cold, his jaw set. "Where is Daoud now?"

"He has many places in West Beirut. When he didn't return from his office tonight, I called them all. He is in the penthouse of a building that the bank owns on Avenue Ramlet El Baida overlooking the sea, number Eighty-one." She leaned back in the chair, a self-satisfied smile curving her lips. "Now, the rest of my money."

Saif shook his head. "No," he replied, "he will be wary. I need you to get us into the flat. Go back to the flat you share with Daoud. Pack your things. Bring them with you and meet me in the lobby of the El Baida place in two hours."

The alarm was evident on her lovely face. "No, I can't do that."

"If you want the rest of your money you will do it. I

need your voice to get him to open the door."

Rabani Saif stood. His face as he leaned over the woman was impassive, as if the skin was pulled so tight over his skull that there wasn't enough elasticity to allow for expression.

"Daoud must die. You, Marie Boulard, will help me kill him. If you don't, the woman, there at the bar, will kill you."

Without another word he walked away, nodding at Yushi Nuhr as he passed.

She joined him on the narrow sidewalk. "Well?"

"It is true. Daoud is a traitor. The Israelis know everything."

He gave her instructions and hurried to the car. His two bearded bodyguards were already in the front seat.

"Ali, get the other car. Head into the valley and tell Hashan that we have been betrayed to the Israelis. They plan some kind of an operation tonight. Warn him."

Without a word the man in the passenger seat left the car and disappeared into the darkness.

"Take me back to the safe house," Saif said. "I have to get on the radio to London at once."

The car lurched forward. Saif leaned back in the seat and tried to arrange the jumbled thoughts in his mind.

Hashan Akbar would have set the missiles by now, and completed the codes that would detonate them. As per their agreement, Akbar would be sending the codes to him, Rabani Saif, and to General Yassar in Jordan.

Whatever the Israelis planned, Saif could only hope that Hashan Akbar got those codes distributed so that at least one of the three of them had them, no matter what the Israelis planned.

One of the three had to go ahead with the Jordan Plan even if the other two were dead.

TWO

The party was at Reba Wallace's huge, posh Belgravia flat. It was small by her standards, about seventy-five people. All but one of the seventy-five had received a handwritten invitation.

The seventy-fifth was a gate-crasher. His name was Nick Carter. Twenty-four hours earlier, the chief of AXE had been abrupt if not specific in ordering Carter to London.

"It's something called the Jordan Plan, and we think it's right out of left field," David Hawk had said. "So far out that a few people on the far right in Tel Aviv might be able to use it to invade Lebanon again."

"And you think Reba Wallace knows about it?" Carter had asked.

"With her hidden Beirut connections, it's almost a sure thing that her intelligence network knows all about it. We want to know something, Nick. Bump into her, renew an old friendship. Let nature take its course."

Carter thought of Hawk's last line, and smiled as he looked out over the crowded room.

The things he didn't do for the service.

But prying information out of Reba Wallace was actually a pleasurable perk of the job.

Tonight's crowd looked like a good blend of the diplomatic group, the theater world, and a few aging hippies.

Several guests were nuzzling drinks, their voices filling the high-ceilinged room with laughter and inane chatter. A tall blonde with long bangs and tanned legs in a thigh-high skirt stood by the bar. As the bartender frowned, she swirled her own martini in a cocktail pitcher with practiced hands.

The swirling stopped when Carter reached the bar. "My, my, where did you come from?" she cooed.

"New York."

"Wonderful, a fellow American! Have a martini?"

"No thanks. Scotch." The barman went to work.

"Have both. I'm Clarisse." She smiled warmly.

"Nick."

"Hi, Nick. I'm an aging widow. How about you?"

"Just passing through," Carter said, grabbing his scotch and moving into the crowd.

The more he circulated, the more he saw the separationist aspects of the party. One side of the room looked like a hairdressers' convention, all movement. The other side looked like a collection of wax figures from Madame Tussaud's.

He was about to ask someone where the hostess was, when a hand slid into his from behind and a breathy voice whispered in his ear.

"I don't remember inviting you, Nick, but I would have had I known you were in town."

Carter knew the touch of the hand and the voice. He turned slowly, without moving away, so their bodies almost touched.

"Hello, Reba. I just dropped by for a drink."

"Of course you did."

She was gorgeous and she lost nothing in a six-inch closeup. She had honey-dark hazel eyes under heavy lids, fine nostrils that flared up with each breath, and full, sensuous lips. Sable hair with just the right red hue flowed untidily to her shoulders.

From the shoulders down she was all woman in a crimson gown that hugged every curve. It was as if she had been sewn into the dress.

"You look hungry," she chuckled.

"Oh, I am."

"Food? The buffet is over there."

"No, thanks. I had Chinese on the way over."

Reba was about to speak again, when something about five-seven with foggy eyes and wavy, corn-colored hair moved in and slid an arm around her waist.

"Excuse me," he said to Carter, and stood on his toes to kiss Reba on the cheek. "Darling, I have the new patterns for Brighton. Why don't we drive down in my Rolls after this awful bash, and we'll go over them together in the morning?"

As he spoke his hand crawled up her side to her left breast.

"You know I can't do that, Godfrey. Business in the morning."

"Oh, posh, that's all you do lately . . . business, business, business," he said, pouting. "You're always on the phone. But I must admit, I do adore female tycoons."

Now his hand had a firm grip on as much of Reba's left breast as he could cover. Carter smiled over his scotch until Reba deftly pried his fingers loose and held his hand.

"Godfrey, I'd like you to meet Nick Carter. Nick, Godfrey Chambers. Godfrey is doing the designs for my new Brighton house."

Godfrey dropped a limp hand into Carter's paw. "I only do the very best houses. And you?"

"I don't do houses," Carter said.

"Oh, I know that. Your line?"

"I'm a wiseguy," Carter said.

"What?"

"I'm in the Mafia."

"Oh, really?" The eyebrows arched and Carter was given a head-to-toe appraisal. "Yes, I suppose you might be. You have that look," he said, then turned back to Reba. "Darling, excuse me for a moment, will you? Nature calls, you know."

Godfrey scooted away and Reba chuckled. "You really shouldn't have done that, you know. He has a dreadful fear of men as it is."

"It seems every time I meet you there are one or two of his type hanging on tight."

She shrugged. "They're harmless and they don't get involved . . . if you know what I mean."

"I know what you mean," he replied with a grin, and took her by the elbow. "Let's dance. I want to whisper sweet nothings in your ear."

Pressed close, Carter was aware of every contour of her body. He moved his lips close to her ear and let the scent of her hair invade his nostrils.

"Why are you in London, Nick?" she asked abruptly.

"To see the Queen."

"Touché." She pursed her lips. They were glistening with bright red gloss. "Then why are you at my party?"

"To see you."

"According to my ears in the City, you've been in town twice in the last year and you haven't even called me. What's so special about this time?"

"Please, Reba," he said, putting all the pain he could muster into his voice, "I'm supposed to wine you, dine you, seduce you into a warm bed, and then try to get every scrap of information possible out of you during pillow talk."

Her head went back with a husky laugh and Carter kissed the fine, white column of her throat as emphasis.

"I'll say one thing, Carter, you're honest."

"Only with people who have saved my skin a time or two," he replied dryly.

"All right, to the terrace."

Arm in arm, they moved through the French doors onto the moonlit terrace. For the moment they had it to themselves. Carter steered her to the rail. In the distance they could see the Thames flowing toward the sea. The lights on the bridges across the river were like diamonds on soft velvet.

"I love London in the fall."

"Yeah," Carter growled, "it's grand."

"You have no romance in your soul, Nick."

"Bullshit. I have lots of romance. Business first, romance later."

Nevertheless, he reached for her hand and felt her fingers close over his.

"How much do you already know?" she murmured.

"Not much," he admitted. "It's something called the Jordan Plan. Evidently it was hatched by some hotheads, and could have far-reaching implications. Our person in Beirut says you're on to it and probably on the edge of doing something about it.

"We are." She glanced down at the diamond-encrusted platinum watch on her wrist and curled under his arm. "In fact, we should have it all wound up in about two hours, four at the most. Make a deal with you . . ."

"Like what?"

"I show you the etchings in my new Brighton digs, buy you a drink or two . . ."

"You're not following the scenario. I'm supposed to be seducing *you*."

"You did that last time, now it's my turn." She smiled. "Where are you staying? I'll have your bags picked up."

Carter grinned. "My bag is in your foyer closet. I brought it with me in the cab."

She tried to slap him but he caught her wrist and kissed her instead.

Since they were in no rush, Carter took the smaller A23 out of London and avoided the more crowded main highway. The sky was still clear and it looked as though it would stay that way all the way to Brighton.

Reba had changed clothes for the drive as soon as she was able to sneak away from her guests. In the long, figure-hugging crimson gown she had conveyed the image of exactly what she was: a wealthy, beautiful woman of the world. Between her diamonds, the dress, and an inherent haughty manner, she had appeared like an ice maiden.

Now, with her long legs curled beneath her body in the passenger seat, she looked girlish and eminently desirable. The black skirt pulled tight to outline full thighs and ripely flared hips. The suit jacket was open, and the white silk blouse lifted and fell with the movement of her high, firm breasts.

"Comfortable?"

She glanced at him and her red lips widened in a wry smile. "As comfortable as I can be in a mini-car."

"It is not a mini-car, my darling. It is a very fine Ford four-door Cortina."

"It's not my Rolls."

"It will do you good to rough it now and again," he chided her.

She lit two cigarettes and passed one to him with a good-natured laugh. Carter had insisted that they take his rental car from the Belgravia flat. Later, if he had to move fast, he didn't want to be worried about getting a Rolls-Royce back to her.

They drove another five miles in silence, Carter glancing up every few seconds at the rearview mirror. That time of evening, most of the traffic past Gatwick Airport consisted of eighteen-wheelers, oil trucks, and an occasional police car. That was why Carter was able to spot the green four-door Jaguar. At first he didn't really consider it a tail because it had dropped back as much as three or four miles several times. When he realized that each time the Jaguar dropped back, an equally high-powered Rover took its place, he knew they had a problem.

"Is there a decent road we can cut off on up here soon?" he asked, watching yet another shift in the two cars behind him.

Reba gave him a blank stare for a moment, and then nodded. "Just before Crowley you can cut to the right on the A264. Why?"

"Don't look now," Carter replied, "but I think we've got company."

Reba's body froze. Finally, after another mile, she asked, "Are you sure?"

"I'm not positive, but if they both follow me when I cut off, I think we'll know."

"'They'? There's more than one?"

He nodded, putting a little more lead in his foot. "Two cars, a green Jag and a gray Rover. Can't tell for sure, but I think there are two men in each car."

"What do you think, you or me?"

He shrugged. "Offhand, I'd say me. Moscow's had a price on my head for a long time. So far they haven't tried to collect it because of the retaliation. Who knows? Maybe they decided suddenly it's worth it."

A sign came up, CROWLEY 1. Just beyond it was a crossroads warning for the A264, with HORSHAM just beneath it.

"How big is Horsham?"

"It's not a village. It's . . . maybe forty thousand people."

"Good. Hang on."

Carter took the right turn without any slackening in speed, and floored the Cortina the moment the car was straight again. He got it up to a good fast clip, but in a flat-out road race with either of the bigger cars, he knew they wouldn't have a chance.

"Any lights?"

"None yet," she replied.

The road was narrow, no lights, only the moon when it decided to slip out from behind the occasional cloud. Instead of hedgerows, good-sized trees lined the road, many of them meeting. They would make it harder to see the trailing cars even with the moon.

He came up fast on a big truck spewing diesel fumes. There was another coming hard from the other direction. Carter dropped a gear and swung out to pass. Just in time he slid between the trucks.

In the rearview he saw a light dart out from behind the truck.

"There's a car there."

"I see it," Carter said. "Have you ever used this road?"

"A few times. There's a road soon that will take you to the village of Field Place, if you want to avoid Horsham."

He saw the other car swing in behind them and come on fast. Behind it, the second car passed the truck.

No pretense now, Carter thought. They were coming on and they were letting him know it.

"Have you got a gun?" he asked casually.

"A gun? My God, Nick, this is England!"

"And you're insulated by wealth, my dear, but you're still a top agent for Mossad . . ."

He got no further. The Rover was swinging out to overtake him, and the driver of the Jaguar was speeding up to take the Rover's place. They were going to cut him off and try a squeeze play.

Suddenly Carter dropped his foot off the accelerator. Behind him, the Jaguar had to hit his brakes. The Rover shot up alongside them. Just as the front of the bigger car got past the Cortina's rear, Carter swerved hard into it.

Between impact and instinct on the part of the Rover's driver, Carter won round one.

The Rover skidded off the road and slid sideways into a grove of trees.

"You did it!" Reba shouted.

"Yeah, down but not out . . . and here comes number two."

He dug into the shoulder rig under his left armpit and pulled Wilhelmina, his 9mm Luger, from her resting place.

"You remember how to use this?"

"Of course."

"Then here," he said, passing it over. "You probably won't hit them, but that's not important at this point."

She smiled. "I'll hit something."

"Just don't take chances. Don't even stick your nose out to see if you are firing in the right direction. Just roll down your window, stick the gun out, and fire to the rear."

Reba's moxie took over; she did what he asked. She managed to hit a headlight on the Jaguar. If only she could hit the other one!

"I'm empty."

Carter dug in his jacket and passed her a fresh clip. "Are there any bad curves up ahead?"

She concentrated on the road for a second, and nodded. "There's an S-turn about half a mile on, first to the right and then to the left. Right between the two turns there's an old abandoned barn very close to the road on the right."

"Good enough—be ready for it. In the meantime, give 'em some more hell."

Carter floored the Cortina as Reba started firing again. Surprisingly, the men in the other cars hadn't fired back. One of her shots shattered the windshield on the left side of the Jaguar. The car weaved wildly and came on faster, catching up to their insane speed and almost snagging the Cortina's rear bumper.

Instead of fighting it, Carter went with it, letting the car drift right into the first turn. The Jag's driver was good with his hands but a little slow with his eyes and mind.

Too late he saw the second curve come up. Carter jammed the brakes in the middle of it and the Jaguar shot past.

The driver tried to correct, but he was too late. The Jag sideswiped the old barn and spun crazily across the road. It rolled one complete turn quickly, then started a second one slowly to end up on its roof against the trees.

Carter was by the Jaguar before it settled. Purposely he took the bypass around Horsham and took an older, even smaller road south. The sides of this road were hedgerowed right up to the pavement. There was little doubt that the Rover was back in action and would probably be on them soon. But with Carter straddling the center line they wouldn't be able to pass and crowd him.

"How far to the A24 south?" he asked.

"About eight miles."

He handed her the last clip from his jacket pocket. "Reload!"

Her hands worked on the Luger with deft concentration. "Why are you slowing down?"

"So they can catch us," he replied, taking the loaded Luger from her and jamming it between his legs.

She didn't answer.

They were about two miles from the A24 when Carter saw the curve he wanted. Just around it, the road widened. He pulled to the side of the road and killed his lights. Then he pulled the emergency blinkers on and started to get out of the car.

"Nick, what the hell are you doing?" Reba cried.

"Stay below the window, luv. I'm going to check the oil."

"Oh, my God."

He lifted the hood, braced it, and put the upper half of his body into the engine compartment.

"Nick, this is crazy!" Reba hissed.

"Not really. We'll have surprise here, and didn't you mention earlier that the final papers haven't been registered yet on the Brighton house?"

"Yes."

"Then I don't see much sense in leading them right to it. Have faith, luv."

He heard the Rover downshift into the curve, but didn't move as the light sprayed half his body and the Cortina. Just as he had hoped, they were going too fast to stop at once.

The tires screamed as the Rover sailed past the Cortina. It was a good fifty yards until they finally got the big car stopped. By that time Carter was sprinting toward them, coming up on their blind side.

He held his fire as the doors opened. He counted four of them spilling out of the Rover. That meant the two in the Rover had stopped long enough to pick up the other two in the Jaguar.

They scarcely hit the ground when they spotted him. This time they weren't going to bother trying to make it look like a driving accident. The two coming out the driver's side had machine pistols and they started firing the moment they spotted Carter's darting figure.

A slug sailed past his head and ricocheted off the hood of the Cortina behind him. As the second and third shots whistled around Carter, he dropped to one knee and aimed at the nearest white shirt.

He squeezed the trigger of the Luger twice in rapid succession. The patch of white turned dark and spread as the man stumbled forward holding his chest. His eyes were bugged wide open, and stayed that way as a third slug from the Luger smacked into his forehead and he crashed backward into the hedgerow.

Immediately, Carter took a sideward roll and fired at the second man flattened out on his belly. The Luger put a slug into the man's throat and he was dead before he hit the ground.

Carter used elbows and knees to wriggle his way to the side of the car, staying in a prone position.

The two on the other side were confused, one toward the rear, stationary, and one toward the front, moving cautiously.

Carter took aim and shot the one coming around the front of the car. His scream was followed by the clatter of his automatic hitting the pavement and then him, clutching his leg.

Carter swiveled the Luger around toward the legs of

the one just across from him toward the rear of the car.

"I can see you, bastard, and you can't see me. Drop the gun!"

The man dropped the gun as he was told, but he didn't stay put.

As Carter was coming to his feet, the man jumped to the roof of the car. His feet had barely made contact with the metal when he leaped again, over the hedge-row.

Carter could hear his feet pounding over the pasture on the other side. In the darkness it would be foolhardy to try following him.

Then he heard it, the sound of metal scraping across the pavement. He dropped to his belly just in time to see the wounded man leveling his automatic.

His intent was clear. He meant to dish out the same poison to Carter by shooting away his legs.

The Killmaster shot first. The slug made a neat hole in the top of the man's forehead.

Quickly, Carter checked the bodies for identification. He found none, but he hadn't expected that he would.

That didn't leave him completely ignorant. All of them had the same skin coloring, dark hair, and dark mustaches.

They could be Spaniards, of course, or Sicilians, or even Israelis.

Carter guessed they were Arabs.

He started to shoot out the front tires, and then thought better of it. Somewhere on the other side of the hedgerow, the live one was probably waiting to see what he would do.

Let him clean up the mess, Carter thought, and headed back to the Cortina.

Reba was lying down in the front seat smoking a cigarette.

"You're filthy."

"It's dirty work," he replied, and slid into the driver's seat.

As he turned the car around, neither of them said aloud what was on their minds.

Was this team after him?

Or her?

Or both of them?

THREE

They landed, eight of them in a cove just south of the Summerland Hotel. Their faces were blackened and they wore dark camouflage fatigues along with night glasses.

Each of them carried silenced Uzis and holstered 9mm Parabellum M1951 Berettas, also silenced. All of them had walkies for short-range communication. One man carried a field radio that would reach back into Israel to give a report on the outcome of the evening's raid, as well as checking with the other team on their mission far north in the downtown section of West Beirut.

They had come in from a passing freighter aboard a rubber raft with a small, one-horsepower motor. Minutes after hitting the beach, the raft and the motor were buried.

Now, on darkened, uninhabited back streets, they jogged through the inky night. The buildings around them were mere shells, destroyed during the civil war or the later Israeli invasion.

They were the Blue Group, under the command of Captain Matti Bazri. Their target was the underground command headquarters of Hashan Akbar, located halfway between the city limits of Beirut and the international airport to the south.

Their mission was the complete termination and the retrieval of all documents, microfilm, or recorded matter concerning the project code-titled "Jordan Plan."

The men jogged along easily, covering mile after mile without so much as a heavy breath between them. A twenty-mile run for their commando team was an everyday occurrence.

Tonight's run would be only sixteen kilometers, a little more than nine and a half miles.

When the lights of the Palestinian Red Crescent Society Hospital gleamed on their left, Bazri gave a hand signal and the eight men veered right. When the scattered lights of the Burj Al Barajinah refugee camp shone ahead of them as a beacon, they slowed.

"Two kilometers," Bazri said. "Fan out. You know the hill and the house. I'll give the signal on the walkie. Red to green is go, and it means go *now*! And, remember, no noise."

Within seconds, the other seven men had become muted shadows in the darkness.

Bazri gave them thirty seconds and moved forward himself.

Julian Daoud sat on the balcony eight floors in the air watching the milky illumination from the moon float across the calm Mediterranean Sea.

That was to his left.

To his right was the bombed-out shell of his beloved Beirut. He listened to the sounds below him, and found them few compared to the sounds of his youth, when Beirut was the Paris of the Med.

In those days, boys hawked the city's twenty-four daily newspapers and citizens gobbled them up to argue hotly over the two-dozen versions of the same lies. The cobbled back alleys of the souks rang with their voices.

Daoud laughed aloud.

Beirutis enjoyed arguing nearly as much as they enjoyed making money.

Julian Daoud missed the old Beirut.

Was he right in thinking that by helping the Israelis he could bring it back?

But did he have any choice?

Would it have been better to accept poverty than to turn against his Arab brothers?

Or *was* he turning against them?

No, he thought not. Julian Daoud looked upon himself as a visionary, just as his father had been.

Julian Daoud had never been poor, and accumulating money held no particular fascination for him. His father had been a banker as well, equally adept at besting the French and the Arabs during colonial days. His father had learned the art of business from his father, a caravan trader who'd begun with camels and later converted to trucks bought on the black market from French army motor pools.

Accumulating money, Daoud believed, was for those who needed it to buy things . . . to acquire things. To make money you had to be smarter than the other man who wanted to make it. Luckily, most men wanted to accumulate it, which always gave you the advantage. They saw money as a personal thing, a means of life and existence . . . a woeful disadvantage.

Daoud saw money and power as a way of rebuilding his beloved Beirut.

That was why, when his fortune had been on the verge of collapse, he had accepted the offer of aid from his father's friend, the powerful French Jew, Isser Wallace. Only later did he realize what strings were attached. Isser Wallace was as powerful in the Mossad as he was in world finance.

"Julian, accept it. Israel and the Israelis are there. They have the land and they will keep it. Making more war will not drive them out, nor will it return Beirut and Lebanon to its former glory. Help us, and we will help you."

And so they had.

Daoud had become an Israeli informer in Beirut. And when old Isser had died and his beautiful daughter had stepped in to take his place, Julian Daoud had worked just as hard for her.

Now he was happier than ever for his choice. Because of it, those three maniacs, Hashan Akbar, Rabani Saif, and the Jordanian, Aman Yassar, wouldn't have a chance to put their insane plan into action and throw the whole Mideast into yet another long, bloody war.

With these thoughts in mind, Julian Daoud fetched his pot of coffee and egg-sized cup on a tray to the balcony. He set the tray on a glass-topped table. A fitful breeze came in from the sea, prompting him to gather his black silk robe more tightly around himself.

Or was it the breeze that had given him a sudden chill?

He checked the Rolex that Reba Wallace had given him for his last birthday. The two Israeli assault teams would be in place somewhere out there in the dark Lebanese night. And somewhere near Amman, in Jordan, a lone assassin would be stalking General Aman Yassar.

Within the hour—two hours at most—it would be over.

With a shudder, Daoud sat down and poured himself a cup of coffee. He slurped it in the timeless Arab manner. It clung to his tongue like syrup and he savored the acrid sweetness of it.

He was about to pour a second cup, when the bell shattered the even silence of the apartment.

Immediately, Daoud's round body began to shake.

Who could be ringing the bell at this time of night? Moreover, who could be ringing *this* bell? The flat was registered as empty. He kept it that way for just this sort of emergency.

Again the sharp chime that shattered his nerves.

Daoud moved to the door. He was safe. Eight floors up and the door was solid steel with a wood veneer.

"Yes, who is it?" he whispered.

"Julian, it is me, Marie."

"Marie, I told you to stay in the other flat!" he hissed.

"I was lonely," she whined. "Let me in, Julian. I don't want to sleep alone tonight."

Daoud sighed. He had never married. His father had taught him that two commitments invariably compromised each other. "An angry wife can bankrupt you," that wise man had said more than once. So Daoud's one "wife" had remained money.

But his flesh needed a woman, and through the years he had taken mistresses, four of them. The latest was once his secretary. When he had found Marie Boulard's skills in bed a hundred times more accomplished than her skills in the office, he had transferred her.

Shifting the revolver to his left hand, Daoud lifted his right to lift the peephole cover. Marie's beautiful but vacant face stared back at him.

"Please, Julian, I need you tonight," she purred.

With another sigh, Daoud unfastened the three locks and opened the door to admit her.

It was a total surprise. Marie was flung into his arms. His gun hand was thrown wide. He got only a glimpse of the two men who filled the doorway behind her. He never saw the silenced Magnum revolvers in their hands.

Eighteen quiet shots were fired. Over half of them passed through Marie Boulard's body before they went on to kill Julian Daoud.

The house was on a low hill at the end of a narrow lane bordered by young cypress trees. Two aged Renaults and a battered Volkswagen were parked to the side. The hoods of all three cars were still warm. They had just brought the occupants of the house from the Jordanian frontier.

Near the chimney on the tile roof, a weary sentry cradled an AK-47 assault rifle in his arms and wished he had not drawn the first watch after such a strenuous night.

Carefully, he cupped his cigarette with both palms to hide the flame.

It did no good.

The firefly glow of his cigarette was like a laser dot for the Israeli sharpshooter.

The sentry made no sound as he slumped dead against the chimney with the still-lit cigarette drooping from his lips.

Inside, three men lounged around a kitchen table off a small living room. They smoked, drank strong Turkish coffee, and talked in low voices.

There were two small bedrooms in the rear of the house. In one, two men slept soundly, their snores echoing lightly off the windowless walls. Both men sprawled fully clothed across their cots, Russian-made AK-47s at their sides.

In the second bedroom, Leila Samir half-lay, half-sat on the only chair in the room. A half-smoked cigarette dangled from her fingers.

She wore dark green, baggy slacks, a bottle-green blouse, and boots. Her clothes were caked with dust, as was her face.

Beneath the grime she was attractive, almost beautiful. Facially, she could have been a direct descendant of the Egyptian Queen Nefertiti, one of the most beautiful women of history. Even under the twenty-four hours of accumulated dust, sand, and grime, her classical features shone through.

But Leila Samir wasn't Egyptian. She was Palestinian, and she had grown up in the refugee camps in Jordan. Her youth had been spent in cold nights and days with nothing to eat. She had known no sounds but those of wailing and bickering and armies fighting.

Her father was the first to go. He was killed on a raid back into Israel. Her mother simply disappeared.

The United Nations fed her, clothed her, and educated her. Palestinian elders had taken her and other children like her to a hilltop and pointed downward to the rolling land on the other side of the Jordan River.

"That is your land, your birthright. The Jews have taken it from you. For that, you live like a dog. But you are not helpless."

She was eleven when she went to the PLO camp in Lebanon to join the resistance. In the camp she learned to make crude bombs out of gasoline cans and alarm clocks. She learned to kill with her hands, a knife, a gun. She studied sabotage and infiltration and Marxist analysis.

When Leila Samir was fifteen, her beauty and intelligence were noticed by the leaders. She was sent to school in Cuba, where she learned languages and her espionage training was honed. Then it was to Damascus, where she joined Al Fatah and began to kill in earnest.

Eventually she met Hashan Akbar. At the time, he was an officer in Syrian intelligence. Akbar chafed at the do-nothing attitude of the Arab states. He wanted Israel destroyed at any cost. He grew to hate the waiting attitude of his Syrian superiors and his other Arab brothers.

At first, when Akbar told her of the Jordan Plan, Leila Samir was filled with repugnance. She had already seen so much killing—and done so much of it herself —that killing on the scale Akbar proposed sickened her.

But her training, and the fact that she had fallen in love with Hashan Akbar, overcame her common sense. It was Leila Samir who had arranged the original meeting between Aman Yassar, Rabani Saif, and Hashan Akbar.

Out of that meeting had come the Jordan Plan.

Now, three years later, the missiles were in place and the time to act was at hand.

Sweaty and tired, Leila again began to doubt if what they did was right. She knew the Jordanian, Aman Yassar, to be a self-serving pig. Her fellow Palestinian, Rabani Saif, had broken with the PLO to establish his own splinter group of terrorists in Lebanon. Besides being slightly mad, Saif also sought power for himself. And he was not above sacrificing *anyone* to get that power.

And her own lover, Hashan Akbar?

The shower quieted and Hashan Akbar entered the room, naked, drying his body with a filthy towel.

He was tall, with a darkly handsome, broad-cheekboned face. His curly black hair was going prematurely gray at the temples. Leila never noticed it, just as she refused to notice that the light of life had gone from his eyes in the past year. Now, when he stared, even at her, his eyes had the blank stare of the blind.

"Will you wash?"

"Soon," she replied, lifting her eyes.

He dropped the towel to the floor and stretched his big body across the bed. For the briefest of seconds, Leila stared at his nakedness and felt the old stirrings in her own body.

The feeling was brief. She turned away.

She knew that inside Hashan Akbar was a patchwork shell. No spleen, forty or fifty tucks in his intestines where bullets had ripped into him and been sewn up by unbelieving surgeons. A femur held together by a steel plate. And the upper part of his spine, on which his large head rested, a jigsaw puzzle of vertebrae glued together by the medical equivalent of epoxy, after two Christian militiamen had broken his neck with baseball bats and tried to turn his backbone to dust with their boots.

It was then that Akbar had changed. But only recently had Leila discovered it. No longer did he live and fight for the starving women and children in the camps. Now he did it all for his own revenge.

"If you aren't going to wash or undress, then come to bed as you are and turn out the light. You must get an early start to Amman in the morning and I must meet with Saif."

Leila sighed and pushed herself to her feet. She was halfway to the bathroom, when a scream of agony erupted from somewhere in the front of the house and the bedroom door flew open. It was Amani, Hashan's brother, blood pouring from a wound in his side.

"Hashan!" he shouted. "It is the Israelis . . ."

Those were the only words he uttered. Cloth, blood, and gore erupted from the front of his chest as bullets poured into his back. His body tumbled forward to land at their feet.

Akbar rolled from the bed grabbing a rifle in the

same movement. Leila clawed the Beretta from the waistband of her slacks as they both dropped.

Two Israeli commandos filled the door, firing waist high. Slugs from the AK-47 and the Beretta sent them reeling back.

"Quickly, to the basement!" Akbar hissed, already on his feet.

Trained to obey, Leila followed him instantly down the dark hall. At the end was a trapdoor, beneath it a flight of raw wood steps that led down to a cold room for the short storage of meat, milk, and other perishables.

Just as Leila yanked up the trapdoor, the snout of an Uzi was thrust around the corner from the living room. It had barely begun to chatter when Akbar's Russian-made assault rifle barked in response.

"Down!" he hissed.

Leila disregarded the stairs and dropped to the dirt floor. She grabbed the flashlight always kept at the foot of the stairs, and looked up. Akbar fired two more long bursts with the rifle, and came down the steps himself. When she heard the trapdoor slam, she snapped on the flash and gave him light to secure the two heavy steel bolts.

Seconds later, he dropped beside her. "Hurry, help me with the vat!"

Together they lifted a heavy wine cask off its cradle away from the wall. Behind it was a round hole just big enough to crawl through.

"Go!" he hissed.

Leila hesitated. "What about you?"

"No. Just you. Leila, you have the new locations of the missiles, the frequencies, and the sequence for the detonators. Use only back streets. If you have to hide, do it in bombed buildings or the sewers. Get the information to Julian Daoud. He'll find a way to relay it to Aman Yassar and Saif."

"But you . . . ?"

"I am dead. The plan must come off. They'll suspect the tunnel if someone isn't down here firing at them."

Suddenly there was pounding from above and one slat of the thick trapdoor cracked.

"Axes!" Akbar said, and fired a burst toward the door. "Go!" he cried.

She paused for only an instant, then moved toward the mouth of the tunnel.

"Leila . . ."

She turned. He leaned forward and kissed her gently on the lips. Leila could feel tears sting her eyes. They were the first tears she had shed since she was a child. It was the first time he had kissed her in over a year.

"I did love you, Leila. Now go."

He lifted her bodily and slid her into the tunnel. Immediately she began slithering. The tunnel was nearly a mile long and it came out in the rear of a garage. In the garage, a motorcycle was always gassed and waiting, ready for just this sort of eventuality.

Only once did Leila crane her head over her shoulder to look back.

Akbar had snapped off the light. Between bursts from his assault rifle, she could hear the axes splintering the trapdoor.

FOUR

The house was at the end of a long drive lined by trees and surrounded by vast, sprawling lawns. Reba informed Carter that the previous owner had built tennis courts and a stable as well as installing a pool, but before he could finish the remodeling of the house itself, his wife and daughter had been killed in an auto accident. Heartbroken, he had given up the project and emigrated to Canada.

All this information had come in a nervous rush throughout the rest of the drive and the late-night snack that had been laid out in the kitchen by the cook.

Carter knew that nonstop talking was Reba's way of avoiding any aftershock from the attack. He let her chatter, and said little himself until the meal was finished and she had poured brandy.

"How many servants?"

"Two," she replied, "gardener and cook. They came with the house."

"Where do they stay?"

"In the pool house."

"Any dogs?" he asked.

"No."

"Jesus, Reba, you're a sitting duck," he growled. "At least in Belgravia you have an alarm system."

"I can't be bristling with bodyguards all the time," she snapped. "My cover is good and that would blow it!"

Carter backed off. "Are the telephones secure?"

She nodded. "That was the first thing I did. And any important calls are jammed at both ends."

He lit a cigarette. "You want to give me the whole story now?"

Again she consulted her watch. "Soon, Nick, I promise. Orders. You'll have to relay to Washington the minute I tell you, and I know it. Let our people do the job, then I'll tell you all, I promise."

She moved around the table and brushed his lips with hers. At the same time, she did wild things with her fingers on the back of his neck. So much so that when she made her next suggestion he found himself agreeing with a smile.

"There's nothing either of us can do about it for at least another two hours," she purred. "So, for the next two hours, what say we just be us?"

"You mean human?... with all the cares, desires, and lusts of—"

"Damn you," she said, laughing, "don't go Shakespeare on me . . . just human!"

"Deal," he said, reaching for her.

"I must make one small phone call, to give them this number. Give me about ten minutes, all right?"

"No more."

"The master suite is at the top of the stairs, first door on the right."

Her heels tap-tapped out of the kitchen. When he heard them on the stairs, Carter took his brandy and went outside.

The house was large, real Tudor with oak timbering.

He guessed from the Elizabethan bay windows that it was about four hundred years old. The cost he couldn't even calculate. But then cost, for Reba Wallace, meant nothing. What she wanted, she bought.

He often wondered if she had followed in her father's footsteps in his work for the Mossad out of loyalty to the old man, or a strong belief in the Israeli cause.

He had never asked her. In actual fact, he didn't think he wanted to know. Also, she might begin asking him the same kind of questions, and long ago he had given up trying to search within himself to find reasons for what he did.

It was a job, and the only good end of it was survival.

He made a walking tour of the grounds, and growled in disgust when he realized that if a second team was sent in, they could be in the house before any alarm was sounded.

He reentered the house and secured the rear door behind him. Grabbing the bottle of brandy, he climbed the stairs.

The master suite was what he had always imagined master suites to be before taxes. Under the timbered ceiling was a quantity of fine old hand-carved furniture, including a magnificent dower chest probably two hundred years old. It stood out against plain oyster-pink wallpaper and wall-to-wall carpeting of the same hue. The wide twentieth-century bed struck an incongruous note. A pink silk eiderdown covered its blankets and sheets.

Reba's voice came to him through an open door at the far end of the vast room. "I'm in here. There's a robe in the closet by the door."

Carter tossed his clothing on a chair and found the

robe. It was silk, a garish red, and extended clear to the floor.

The bathroom had black-tiled walls and all black accessories. The modern, sunken tub was three times wider than the norm, and a good ten feet long. Foamy bubbles obscured the water and all of Reba except her naked shoulders and dark head.

"Plenty of room," she said with a grin, lifting a dripping arm and curling her fingers in a come-hither gesture.

"I can see that," he chuckled. "Are you bathing or swimming?"

"Luxuriating, darling," she said sweetly, and added, just as sweetly, "Will you please get your ass in here?"

Carter dropped his robe to the floor and crawled in beside her.

They scarcely spoke. At first they lay still, enjoying the feel of the warm water on their skin and the jasmine smell of the bath salts she used. Later they soaped each other, her body moving sensually under his hands. They kissed then, holding each other's wet body.

Lightly, her fingers traced the scars on his legs, his belly, and his shoulders. "How many more of those do you think you can get before it's the last one?"

"I thought we weren't going to talk about that."

"You're right."

Again they fell silent. It was a long time before Carter spoke.

"How much money do you have?"

She blinked, then shrugged. "I don't really know. Twenty, maybe twenty-five million pounds. You?"

"Ten, maybe fifteen thousand dollars," he replied.

She grinned. "Want to marry me for my money?"

"The thought has crossed my mind, several times."

She shook her head. "You would be bored. Money, *great* money, creates boredom."

"I don't think you're bored."

"No, because I always remember what my father always told me. He said, 'If you live in the wine cellar already built, don't let it make you forget what to do with the grape.'"

Carter thought about this for a moment and turned to her. "And all this is the wine cellar . . . and Israel is the grape. Right?"

"I thought we weren't going to talk about that."

"Right."

This time he kissed her.

She began to moan deep in her throat as his tongue explored. Her heavy breasts filled his hands, overflowing them. He massaged the nipples gently with his thumbs, and her body began to move against his.

Without words between them, Carter got out of the tub and then lifted her to stand beside him. Wordlessly, they patted each other dry with two enormous towels. Then he carried her into the bedroom.

He placed her on the bed and gently lay down beside her. Her arms and lips found him again in silent passion. At first the kisses were tender. Then her breathing became deeper and he felt her breasts heaving against him.

He kissed her hungrily and her tongue slid into his mouth as she caressed his face with her hands. Her inner thighs were like velvet. She clung to him, her eyes closed, and whimpered softly as he caressed her. When he touched the very core of her, she shivered and suddenly clamped his hand with her knees. She let her head loll far back, her eyes open now, staring.

"Now?" he murmured huskily.

"I thought you'd never ask," she whispered.

Then there was no hesitation on either side, no restraints left over from the past; they were simply two people meeting willingly on common ground, and with common need.

He pressed her softness slowly, and she arched her back to meet his thrust.

"Ohhh, God . . . good!" she cried.

He began to move and she picked up the rhythm. In a minute or so they were making the bed shake. She was a bundle of wildcat energy.

He felt her belly touch his. It was soft, flat, and smooth as satin as she arched toward him. He felt the round curves of her breasts heaving. With a cry of strangled lust, he eased her back onto the bed and his strong body covered hers.

She cried out in pleasurable pain when he entered her in long, thrusting movements. Again she threw her hips upward, arching her back and sending her body up to meet his thrust. Deeper into her he went, his mind reeling, his breath fast and heavy. He moved faster, determined to extinguish the burning sensation and unleash the flames of passion in the beautiful body writhing and waiting in anticipation beneath his own.

"More . . . more!" she begged over and over again.

He felt the heat of lust rising from her body to join his own. Both their bodies were already soaked with perspiration. Hearing her cry for more of him made his strokes more savage in their intensity.

Then he felt her passionate release carry her above and beyond fulfillment. Just as her spasms started to subside, he felt the throbbing, fiery freedom of his own release.

She sensed his bursting flood and added to his pleasure by again arching herself toward him, grinding her hips against him, taking all of him, until they both were completely spent, satiated.

Carter finally let sleep swallow him as he felt her lips nibble at his ear.

FIVE

It had taken nearly twenty minutes to chop a large enough hole in the trapdoor so they could put a deadly spray of fire from their Uzis into the basement room. Now they were chopping the rest of the door away so they could make an identification and get a total of the dead.

As this was being done, Captain Matti Bazri was going through the briefcase they had found in the rear bedroom. He had already instructed his radioman to contact the Red Team to get a status on their raid of Rabani Saif's headquarters in downtown Beirut.

"Captain . . ."

"Yes, Sergeant?"

"We've broken through. It was Akbar himself in the basement room."

"Dead?" Bazri asked, examining the last document in the case.

"Yes, sir."

"What's the count then?"

"Seven men dead. Captain . . ."

The tone in his sergeant's voice jerked Bazri's head up. "What is it?"

"There was a tunnel in the basement room, Captain. We think the woman, Leila Samir, escaped that way."

"Shit," Bazri hissed, slamming the last of the papers back into the case and shutting it. "It's all here, the whole plan, except the location of the missiles and their arming and detonating sequences. And we've let the woman slip through our fingers!"

The young sergeant's face paled. "You think that the woman . . ."

Bazri nodded. "I'd stake my life on it. She's got the information in her head."

"Should I send two of the men?"

"No," Bazri said, "too dangerous now. We'll have to use our undercover people in Beirut to get her before she can pass the information on. Besides, we're on deadline now at the rendezvous. What's our status?"

"One man dead, Stein. Tobah is hit bad. We've stopped the bleeding. He'll probably make it."

"Get them both ready to travel. We'll move out in ten minutes."

"Yes, sir."

Carrying the briefcase, Bazri moved into the living room where his radio operator had set up. "Well?"

"Red Team is already on withdrawal, sir. They took no casualties, and left four dead in the apartment."

"Did they get the material?"

"Yes, sir, but our intelligence must have goofed."

"How so?" Bazri asked.

"They didn't get Rabani Saif. He wasn't in the apartment or the surrounding area."

Bazri cursed again. "Get on to Tel Aviv. Tell them our status. And tell them I don't have the locations." He also told the operator to explain in prose code the situation on Leila Samir.

Like the sergeant, the radioman's face paled slightly. "That means she's probably got the final phase of the plan in her head."

Bazri nodded. "Give the go-ahead to terminate Yassar in Jordan. Also, tell Tel Aviv to have our underground people in Beirut alerted about Saif. If Leila Samir can't pass her information on to one of them, we may be able to buy time and find those missiles ourselves."

"Yes, sir."

Captain Matti Bazri hadn't sweated a drop from the beginning of the mission. Now, as he thought of the woman, Leila Samir, out there somewhere, he could feel a river of perspiration running down his back.

General Aman Yassar was unusually tall for an Arab, and unusually heavy. His face bore the ravages of smallpox, a disease that had almost killed him in childhood. His nose, broken by a desperate hashish smuggler with a pistol butt, had never properly healed. The end result was that Yassar presented a fearsome impression, even naked, slipping from the bed of his mistress.

Outside, the sounds of rural Amman, the capital of Jordan, awakening to meet the dawn, reached his ears as he dressed slowly in the dim light.

Today he would arrive early in his offices. Hopefully, the messenger from Beirut would already be there. In a week's time he, Yassar, would be the ruler of Jordan. And, as such, he would dictate the fall of Israel.

He smiled at this as he went down to the street and his car. Soon the entire Arab world would revere Aman Yassar as the man who defeated Israel. To Akbar and Saif, he would give the crumbs. But it would be he, Yassar, who eventually wielded all the power.

The streets around his office already teemed with people going to and coming from the nearby marketplace. He parked his Peugeot in the reserved space and started to fight his way through the hawkers and peddlers to Government Building.

As he moved through the crowd, a man wearing a kaffiyeh and sunglasses came steadily but not menacingly toward him. Yassar looked quickly around him and was not overly surprised to find himself surrounded by people who formed a shifting, sandlike wave. This man, along with others but not with them, simply moved in his direction. They formed an unidentifiable, floating mass in kaffiyehs covering every part of their faces except for the eyes.

"General," the man spoke to him.

"What do you want?" Yassar assumed an authoritative air, but sweat beaded his brow.

Then he saw the pistol.

The chrome silencer caught the sunlight and glittered.

In the background and all around him, shouts, yells, milling people.

"What the hell . . . ?"

"Greetings from Tel Aviv," said the man carrying the pistol, without real expression.

The first shot hit Yassar in the stomach. He felt the breath being squeezed out of him. Then he felt the hot stickiness of blood . . . his blood

"Nooooo!" he gasped.

The second and final shot entered his left eye and exited through the rear of his skull, taking huge wads of brain and hair and skin with it.

The man tucked the pistol inside his robe and moved into the human flow.

Several minutes later, a policeman came upon Yassar. He recognized the suit, the Rolex watch, the gold cigarette case, the physique. The remaining portions of Yassar's face had grown distorted and strangely discolored. The policeman felt nauseated, and had to turn away from the sight of the corpse.

By that time, two other men had completed the task of cleaning out the safe in General Aman Yassar's office.

Ali Naslani parked facing the gates and gave the signal, twice on and off, with his lights.

There was no reply.

Could they all be so fatigued from the mission that they had fallen asleep without posting a sentry?

Quietly, all his senses on the alert, Naslani got out of the car. As he moved through the gate and up the weed-strewn path, he pulled a revolver from under his belt at the small of his back.

"Hashan . . . Amani . . . Leila?" His whispered voice shocked his own senses in the dead stillness.

There was no answer, and Naslani could see the cars under cover at the side of the house. He clamped his jaw tight, and the muscles rippled in his cheeks. He knew he couldn't just stand there and do nothing.

He tried the door. Locked.

He made his way to the rear of the house. Just around the corner, he came to a halt with a gasp. The kitchen windows and the window in the rear bedroom were shattered. He sniffed. There was just the trace of acrid cordite in the air.

Cautiously, he eased his eyes over the rim of the bedroom window. He saw them at once, fully clothed, their rifles still at their sides.

Naslani had killed many times himself, without mercy. But these were his friends. He gagged and then crawled through the window.

He found them, one by one. Some of them were so

riddled with bullets that it took him several minutes to identify them.

The last body he found was in the basement room: Hashan Akbar.

It was another five minutes before he searched the house to his satisfaction. Leila Samir was not among the dead. Somehow, probably through the tunnel, she had escaped.

He hurried back to his car. Rabani Saif would know what to do.

Through back alleys and over the rubble that had once been streets, Leila Samir scrambled. An hour before, she had abandoned the motorcycle. It had proved useless on the route she had to take into Beirut.

She had bypassed the Chatilla refugee camp, and now, as the first gray light of dawn peeked over the horizon, she knew she would never make it all the way north across the city.

In the distance before her, she could hear small-arms fire and, now and then, the roar of a rocket and the blast of a mortar.

She had no way of knowing what was happening. More than likely, one member of one of the many divergent groups had fired on another. Then the second group had fired back, and another mini-war had begun in the southern slums of the Moslem section of already ravaged Beirut.

It was probably the Shiites, either fighting among themselves or against the so-called Syrian peace-keeping force.

In any event, she would never make her way through all the slum areas—Bir El-Abed, Hav Madi, and the densely populated Ghobeiri district—in the coming daylight.

A sniper or a man with a grenade launcher didn't ask his target for allegiances before he fired. In the midst of battle, anyone in the open, on the streets, was a target.

She would have to find cover until nightfall.

Leila used every available scrap of cover, from the shadow of one heap of rubble to another. From behind her and far to her right, as she ran and scrambled forward, bullets slashed the night.

The fear of death showed plainly on her face. But despite her fear and despite the urgent need for speed and freedom of movement, she felt anger and disgust.

Why not? she thought. After weeks of cease-fire, with only an occasional skirmish, why did the fools have to start up another full-scale civil war? From the amount of firing and shelling, she was sure that this was no minor skirmish.

The fools!

It gave her even greater doubts about the information she carried in her head. Without Israel, would these fools still battle among themselves?

Leila Samir could not help but think that they would.

So what good is this great and grand plan?

Around her, assaulting her ears, was the bellowing thunder of war. Before her, the Boulevard Saeb Salaam lay in ruins; pavements gone, gutters gone, the road uprooted, buildings flattened, rubble everywhere . . . all a shambles.

Saeb Salaam had never been beautiful, but it was less than an ugly eyesore now. It had been gaudy with garish neon in days of peace. It had been one café after another, and cheap dance halls with cheaper clientele. It had been the *clack-clack* of high-heeled shoes strutting the pavements throughout the long nights, and whispered invitations from dark doorways. It had been amusement arcades and cut-price jewelers' shops with windows filled with brashly glittering artificial stones. The boulevard had never been beautiful, never distinguished, but now it was a desert.

Leila scrambled on as the bullets whined, seeking safety, looking for shelter and finding none.

On and on she went, now slipping and falling, now staggering to her feet; on and on until the sounds of pursuit were swallowed up in the tumult of the night and bullets searched her out no more. Only then did she pause to take breath.

Behind her, near the Municipal Stadium, she had barely avoided a patrol of five men. She guessed them to be Hezbollah. They had fired at her without even finding out who she was.

She knew the same would apply to any party she met.

At last she reached the boulevard and looked around frantically. Mortars were lighting the sky to her left. She turned right and, almost at once, spotted the door to a cellar half-hidden by mounds of rubble.

It would be a long time until nightfall when she could move again. But anything was better than the open.

As if to underline her thoughts, a machine gun began to chatter nearby. With a cry of alarm, Leila dived into the dark hole.

SIX

A light breeze billowed out the curtain and filled the room with scented night air. Carter awoke, chilled and aware that he was alone in the big soft bed. He lifted himself on one elbow and looked across the room. A figure was sitting quietly in a slipper chair by the window.

Slowly his eyes adjusted and he could see that it was Reba. She had slipped into a thin dressing gown of blue silk and lace. A tray with coffepot and cups sat on an embroidered hassock beside her chair.

Only then did he recognize the aroma that had awakened him.

"Reba?"

"Yes," she answered in a hollow voice.

"What is it?"

Wordlessly, she poured a cup of coffee and carried it to him. She passed him the cup and lit two cigarettes before sitting on the side of the bed.

"It didn't go well," she said. "Tel Aviv contacted me an hour ago. I was instructed to stand by. In the meantime, I was to alert my man in Beirut, Julian Daoud."

"And . . . ?"

"I called Beirut, the safe house where Julian was to wait it out."

"Yes?"

"The telephone was answered by a Syrian intelligence officer."

"Let me wake up," Carter said, squeezing her arm.

He padded to the bathroom and stuck his head under the cold shower. When the cobwebs cleared, he grabbed a towel and the red robe and returned.

She was back by the window, smoking and sipping from her cup. Carter retrieved his own coffee and cigarette and took the other chair.

"Start from the beginning."

"It started a long time ago," she said with a deep sigh. "As near as we can figure, about three years. We had no inkling of all of it, just bits and pieces."

"What kind of 'bits and pieces'?"

"Parts of nuclear-powered missiles were being stolen or bought from all over the world. We learned that they were being smuggled into Beirut, but we could do nothing until we found out why. My man in Beirut—"

"Who?"

"Julian Daoud. He is used often by most of the Arab factions. He has also worked for us for years. His bank is secretly aligned with my French banks. We have agreements."

Carter smiled. "I know."

Reba nodded. "I thought you might. About six months ago, the Palestinian, Rabani Saif, came to Daoud. He laid out parts of a plan that eventually they called the Jordan Plan. It has taken Julian this long to find out everything. About two weeks ago, he finally put it all together, including the principals involved."

Here she paused and moved across the room. Behind a huge tapestry there was an open door. She snapped on a light and Carter could see files and a small radio room, complete with a code teleprinter.

She returned with three manila file folders, and handed them to him. As he glanced through them, she commented.

"The original plan was proposed by a renegade officer in Syrian intelligence, Hashan Akbar. While he was still working in the Syrian government, his job was liaison with practically every terrorist group in the world. He also helped finance and plan several operations. When the word came down from on top that Syria was pulling back because of world opinion, Akbar resigned."

"And took matters into his own hands," Carter muttered.

Reba nodded. "Through his mistress, Leila Samir— there's a file on her and photographs in the rear of Akbar's folder—he got very cozy with Rabani Saif. Together, they came up with the plan. But they needed some access to Jordan and military hardware they hadn't been able to buy or steal."

"Enter General Aman Yassar."

"That's right. Saif and Akbar could be considered idealists. They were truly radical. Yassar is greedy and power hungry. He would like to stage a palace coup and replace Jordan's king. With enough terrorist help, he could probably do it and keep his hands clean. Once that was done, he was also going to be set up as the figurehead to bring Israel to its knees."

Carter yawned. "That seems a little farfetched."

"Not when you see how it was going to be done."

She paused to light another cigarette, and then continued in terse words to explain the basic elements of the Jordan Plan.

The plan was outlandish but simple. Two nuclear missiles were assembled in Lebanon. With Yassar's help, they would be smuggled into Jordan and hidden near the river. Their range would easily reach Haifa and Tel Aviv.

When the missiles were in place, mass demonstrations would occur in Amman, Beirut, and the refugee camps of the Gaza, along with the Arab areas inside Israel. Saif had been organizing these for months by sending in trained agitators.

When the demonstrations were at their peak, the Israeli government would be issued an ultimatum. Agree to a joint Arab-Jewish government in Jerusalem, or most of Haifa and Tel Aviv would be rubble.

Carter interrupted her. "The Israelis would never agree."

"Of course they wouldn't. The next step was to call on all the Arab nations to unite—in fact instead of words—to annihilate the Zionist state."

"And the Arabs wouldn't agree," Carter said.

"No," she replied, "but they would bicker. And while they were bickering, Yassar would make his move in Jordan. Once he gained power, he would instantly endorse the plan. If the other Arab states didn't agree within a certain time period, the missiles would be on their way."

Carter leaned forward. "A fait accompli. The three of them, by using the missiles, would force their fellow Arabs to act."

"Yes," Reba said, nodding, "and act fast. Israel has the bomb. They would use it."

Carter stood and paced. "It's insanity."

"But cunning insanity," Reba declared. "For Saif and Akbar . . . even Yassar, it's the whole loaf or nothing. If they lose, they have still delivered a deadly blow to Israel. If they win, only partially, they might succeed in what has never been done yet, unite the Arab states."

"But the United States . . . England . . ."

"Could do what? Once nuclear bombs are being ex-changed in the Middle East, threats are useless. All the major powers can do is sit back and see who survives. Their major thrust then would be not to let such insanity proliferate."

"Jesus," Carter groaned.

The teleprinter in the radio room started clattering.

She was in there for nearly an hour. While Carter waited, he hit the kitchen. He wasn't that hungry, but he needed to occupy his mind and his hands.

Halfway into the creation of an omelet, he gave it up and settled for half a grapefruit.

Reba was studying a stack of printouts when he got back to the bedroom.

"How bad?"

"Bad," she replied. "The raids were only partially successful. All three sets of the master plan were cap-tured. Hashan Akbar is dead. So is Aman Yassar. They missed Saif in Beirut. That in itself is not so bad."

"Then what is?" Carter asked.

"They found nothing in the captured material about the location of the missiles, or the means of arming and detonating them."

Carter digested this. "Are you sure the missiles are in place?"

"Positive," she said. "The day before yesterday, Akbar took a team into Jordan to mount them and set up the detonating devices."

"But you said Akbar is dead. Did he get that infor-mation to Saif?"

"Not yet, but he might soon."

"How?"

"Akbar's mistress, Leila Samir, escaped in the raid. Tel Aviv is guessing that she has everything in her head.

If she gets to Saif, he can go ahead with the plan."

She paused and took a deep breath. Carter could see, for the first time, that her hands holding the printout were shaking.

"And you can't get in touch with your man, Daoud."

"I have word from Tel Aviv on that as well. Julian and his girlfriend were killed, assassinated. From the sound of it, they were killed about the time the raids were taking place. Since Saif wasn't where he was supposed to be, it could have been him. How he found out about Julian . . ." She shrugged.

Carter went blank. He cleared his mind of everything to concentrate on only the matter at hand. It was several minutes before he spoke again.

"What is Tel Aviv planning?"

"We don't have a top agent in Beirut to handle this. The people we do have are looking for her, but there is another problem. A civil war has started again among the Palestinian factions. The Syrians are not interfering, but there's a lot of fighting in the city."

"Is Tel Aviv going to send anyone in?"

She tried to light a cigarette, but the flame from the lighter wouldn't stay still. "Me."

"What? That's insane!" Carter roared. "If Daoud's dead, they know about you as well. Hell, that party on the road last night . . . now we know *you* were the target, not me."

"Probably."

Carter went to the bar and returned with brandy. He laced a fresh cup of coffee with it and started to pace.

"Nick . . ."

"Shhh. Let me think."

A half hour later he had it all together.

"Even if they know about you, they probably don't know the banking connection to Paris, right?"

"I'm sure they wouldn't."

Carter went on. "And right now, the ones you have to get by to get into Beirut are the Syrians. You'd never make it."

"But you would," she said slowly.

"That's right. And I've got a connection or two that no one knows about in Beirut. How soon can you set me up with your Paris banks to become one of their officers?"

She shrugged. "A few hours."

Carter was already moving. "I'll go commercial from Gatwick, and get a charter out of Orly in Paris. Have your people quietly pull some strings. With Daoud's death, the Paris bankers want someone on top of their money in Beirut. If there's one thing all of them understand, even the Syrians, it's money."

A half hour later, the rented Cortina was flying north toward Gatwick.

SEVEN

The sun burned the last of the morning mist away. Now the sky turned a glaring powder-blue while the sea's green deepened. Traffic snarled and tangled on the streets outside the inner city. Horns blasted ancient people astride donkeys, people from a slower, older day, out of the way. Ships' horns hooted derisively at one another. Barges clanged as they panted in and out of the harbor.

All this while fierce fighting raged in many parts of the city. But even in the souks where bullets whined, merchants called out to sell their morning vegetables. War came and went, but in Beirut there would always be trade.

And in a cellar beneath a bombed-out shop, Leila Samir lay hidden under a pile of empty boxes heaped with sour-smelling, abandoned garbage bags.

She was acutely uncomfortable. The space in which she lay was small and constricted, and the cellar floor was hard and cold. She had agonizing cramps in her legs, yet she could not move. She dared not move. There were other people in the cellar, and they did not know she was there.

When she had found this place and it had been empty, Leila had stumbled down cracked, dust-covered steps and found the piled boxes. Quickly, she had crawled beneath them like an animal seeking somewhere to hide. She had needed sleep badly; she had been terribly tired. But she hadn't been too tired to be careful.

She had known that she couldn't afford to take chances. So she had crawled beneath the piled boxes and arranged them over her, moving them slightly so that no one should know of her hiding place. Then and only then had she permitted herself sleep.

She had awakened to the sound of voices close at hand, and in the first confused moments of wakefulness, knowing the voices to be Arab and being stiff and cramped and in pain, she had even thought that it wouldn't matter to show herself.

These were fellow Palestinians, weren't they? The disembodied voices belonged to Arabs. There could be no doubt of that. They were the voices of men and women speaking in accents that would have proved impossible for the tongue of a foreigner. So why not show herself? Why not move and let the blood return to her arms and legs?

What had she to fear?

These people, if she told them of her mission, would be glad to help her. She had no need to tell them everything.

And then she remembered the beggar near the Sodeco crossing, the one who had pointed out Akbar to the Christian militia. He had accepted a handful of pounds, and then watched calmly as they nearly beat Akbar to death.

The Arab had been a good Moslem, a Palestinian. But he had also been hungry.

Outside, above the chatter of the women in the cellar, Leila could still hear the sound of gunfire. It wasn't nearly as heavy as it had been the night before. But she knew that meant nothing. If anything, it meant that the particular owners of this turf had been driven back and the new occupiers were looting rather than shooting.

Carefully, she opened a hole in the crates. There were three women, one with a small child, and an old man. They were not from this slum area. All of them were well dressed.

From their words and from their appearance, Leila could guess their predicament. Sometime during the night they had been caught on the road when the shooting had begun. They had probably been on their way to the Christian section from the airport, when anything could have happened.

Suddenly their chatter stopped and all heads turned toward the opening to the street.

And then the small world of the waiting, watching people in the cellar exploded into furious noise.

There was shouting, screaming, the sound of shots.

Bullets plowed into the walls and ceiling of the cellar. Chips of cement flew. Plaster fell like rain.

Then suddenly, as quickly as it had begun, the chaos stopped.

Silence, with fear, punctuated the women's faces.

And then Leila knew why. A man, a kaffiyeh on his head, its ends dangling over his chest, moved into her line of vision. His eyes were without pupils and his laugh was a giggle as he prodded one of the women with the barrel of his rifle.

He was on hashish. Leila could see his eyes clearly now, and there was no brain behind them to reason.

He reached out and ripped the front of one of the women's dresses down to her waist. The old man forced himself between them.

"Brother," the old man shouted, "what do you do? We are all one! We know your cause . . ."

A blow from the rifle sent the old man reeling backward. The other two women and the child ran screaming and panic-stricken from the cellar. The remaining woman tried to cover her bare breasts.

As the old man tried to get to his feet, the man with the rifle drew back a heavily booted foot and kicked him full in the face.

The bare-breasted woman screamed and tried to run. A short burst from the AK-47 stitched across her back. She fell against the boxes shielding Leila.

And as she fell, clawing for a life that was already gone, she pulled away Leila's concealment.

Leila stood, her arms at her sides, her hands just behind her thighs. She didn't try to run. It was useless. The AK-47 was pointed at her belly.

The man leered and moved toward her, his free hand rubbing his crotch. When he was close enough, he laid the rifle barrel against her blouse. The material tightened over her braless breasts.

"Brother, I am with Rabani Saif," Leila said calmly. "If you harm me, you will dine on your own balls."

He lifted his hand from his crotch and roughly kneaded her right breast.

She smiled. "Is that the way you would have it, brother?"

"Pretty," he said.

Leila ran her tongue over her lower lip and raised her left hand to her blouse. One by one she unbuttoned the blouse.

His hashish-blurred eyes managed to focus, and drool slobbered from the corners of his mouth. As she unbuttoned the blouse, he moved the barrel of the rifle against the material, baring her breast.

When the muzzle was a good eight inches to her side, Leila raised the Beretta in her right hand and shot him twice in the face.

It took one stop, in Venice. It was set up by the bankers in Paris. It was a matter of baksheesh, a bribe. The procedure was set up by the man who would get the envelope. He was a ranking official in the Syrian embassy in Rome. He would be flying into Venice while Carter was flying in from Paris.

By three o'clock that afternoon, Carter had landed in the chartered jet and took a vaporetto to the Piazza San Marco. Now he sat in a rattan chair in front of a café and nervously watched the afternoon's passing parade.

The contact would be Benji. He spotted a mongrel trotting across the stones, and wondered.

He sipped his strong coffee and concentrated on people instead. A priest in a long black robe and a wide-brimmed black hat hurried past. A few tables away, a group of young American girls were studying maps and guidebooks and counting huge piles of unfamiliar lire as they prepared for another day of sightseeing.

Carter felt a sudden surge of regret that he was not in Venice as a tourist. What a wonderful city for fun. What a lovely day to be carefree and uncommitted, to decide what glass factory or basilica to visit. He sighed without realizing it, finished his coffee, and lit a cigarette.

"Monsieur Villadame? Nicolas Villadame?" A rather thin and high-pitched voice spoke softly beside him.

As Carter looked up, a small dapper man sat down in a chair drawn from a nearby table. He was not now placed at the other table, nor was he quite at Carter's table, but awkwardly in the aisle between.

"May I join you for a moment?"

Nicolas Villadame was a minor clerk in Reba's Paris

bank. His appearance and age had approximated
Carter's. Abruptly, that morning, he had been sent off to
the French West Indies to personally deliver some document.

Carter eyed the little man without expression. *"Oui,
monsieur."*

"My name is Benji. Are you familiar with the name,
Monsieur Villadame?"

"I believe so," Carter replied, "through Paris."

"Quite so," the man replied, his face wreathed in a
broad smile that revealed several gold fillings.

Carter wondered how many of them had been gained
with a percentage of baksheesh.

When the man spoke again, his voice dropped into a
whisper and his dark eyes bored intently into Carter's.
"Leave here now and go to the Grand Canal jetty in
front of the Doges' Palace. Do you know it?"

Carter nodded.

"Wait for a gondola with a red and black cockpit. His
name is Pietro. Speak to him in French. He will know
where to take you."

Without another word he left, walking rapidly toward
one of the narrow streets opening off the piazza.

Carter waited five minutes, paid his check, and
walked to the Church of San Marco. As he passed, the
golden winged lion of Venice struck the hour. A
hundred yards farther on was the Doges' Palace and the
Grand Canal.

He walked out on the stone jetty lying between two
of the ornate lamps that lined the broad promenade beside the canal. A flight of stone steps descended to the
water both to the right and to the left. Lying a few feet
off the lower step of the right-hand flight was the long,
narrow hull of a black gondola. Its battered cockpit was
painted in an odd black and red checkered pattern.

The gondolier, dressed in black trousers and white shirt, stood aft on his platform. He kept the gondola on station in spite of the roughness of the water with just his single oar.

Carter walked down the stone staircase until he stood just above a step covered with green sea lichen and moss over which the rough water lapped rhythmically.

"You are for hire?" he called to the gondolier in French.

"Suo nome, signore?"

"Villadame," Carter replied. "And you?"

"Pietro, signore."

"Good." Carter swung aboard.

Immediately the gondola moved away from the jetty, rolling slightly until the gondolier had it headed into the wind. In five minutes they had moved up the Grand Canal and into calm water.

As they passed a small opening between buildings, the gondola swung sharply to the right and entered it. They glided silently over smooth water down a narrow waterway spanned by occasional wrought-iron pedestrian bridges. In a few minutes they came alongside a gondola that was docked against a narrow walkway parallel to the canal. Its cockpit awning was of deep blue and red striped canvas. Similar canvas drops concealed the interior. As the gondolas touched together, the adjacent canvas drop parted, and a man's firm voice spoke, "Join me here, Mr. Villadame."

Carter stepped from his gondola to the other, and Pietro's boat moved rapidly away. In a moment the gondola in which he was now sitting began to move.

In the gloom and closeness of the shrouded cockpit, he gazed across at a tall, tanned, athletic-looking man with iron-gray hair. The man smiled and put a forefinger to his lips. After a few minutes Carter could tell from the outside sounds that they had reentered the Grand Canal.

Only then did the man speak. "I believe you have an envelope for me, monsieur."

Carter passed a thick envelope over and gave the man a thin-lipped smile. "Ten thousand pounds is a great deal of money."

"Indeed it is, monsieur," the man replied in practically unaccented French. "But your needs are great, especially in the poor, beleaguered country that you wish to enter illegally."

From a briefcase at his feet he withdrew papers and handed them one by one to Carter.

"Here is your visa. You will notice it has a 'Right of Trade' stamp on it. That means you can legally do business. Here is the VIP status letter you requested. Telephone calls have been made. Here are your landing permits. Your pilots and the plane will be allowed to stay in the country only long enough to refuel. Make sure they understand that."

"I will."

"Good. Now, do you have the letter of intent from your superiors in Paris?"

Carter produced it. The man scarcely glanced at it before he took from the briefcase a Syrian seal of state and made the impression.

He handed it back with a broad smile. Carter also smiled. Here was a man of business who knew how to deliver on his baksheesh.

"It was a pleasure doing business with you, monsieur."

The words were barely out of his mouth when the gondolier nestled against a jetty.

Carter stepped from the cockpit without looking back.

An hour later he was in the air over the Adriatic.

Leila didn't wait for nightfall. At dusk she emerged from her cellar and again plied her way through the rubble.

It was by pure luck that she found the basement apartment. It was empty. More than likely its owner was dead or running to a safer part of the city until this new skirmish had run its course.

In a closet she found old, worn clothes. She stripped and donned a rough wool skirt, a dark blouse, and a worn black sweater. There was even a shawl for her head and shoulders that would partially disguise her age.

The meeting with the stoned militiaman had warned her that advanced years in a woman could be a safety factor.

Thick brown cotton stockings and low-heeled shoes completed the costume. The shoes were a size too large, but bits of cloth stuffed in the toes made them almost comfortable.

At the door, she paused. Outside, the shelling had started again in earnest. To the north and east she could hear the chatter of machine guns and small-arms fire. It also seemed worse as evening came than it had in the daytime. It was as if they just kept firing at nothing, randomly, hoping to hit something.

Leila closed her eyes and concentrated on a map of Beirut in her brain.

Directly north of her was hotel row on the Avenue de Paris running along the Mediterranean. It was commonly called Shiek's Row before the fighting, because

all the fine apartment houses and villas of the city were
built there along with the finer hotels.

Julian Daoud's apartment was there, near what was
left of the Hotel St. Georges.

If she went directly north, through the inner city, she
would have to pass through the rest of the densely populated Ghobeiri district as well as the Haret Hreik area.

If her ears were truthful, it was in those districts
where most of the heavy fighting was taking place.

She decided that it would be best to head west, to
Avenue du General de Gaulle and beyond to the
beaches. Once there, the fighting would be little or not
at all. She could make her way then north to the Avenue
de Paris, and east again along the sea.

With any luck, in that area she might even find a
telephone that worked, and be able to call Daoud.

With a shopping basket on her arm, Leila again
moved into the street.

EIGHT

At three hundred miles an hour it didn't take long to traverse the Mediterranean and come up on the coast of Lebanon. From a hundred miles out, the pilot started arguing with the flight controller about landing permission.

Only when Carter got on the mike and read the tower the riot act in French, citing his VIP status directly from a higher authority in Damascus, were they finally given a disgruntled okay.

Lights were coming on as they banked over the city, but it was still illuminated enough to see the range of devastation.

"Bloody grim, ain't it?" the pilot offered.

Carter looked down and agreed. The Paris of the Med had lost her skin and now only the white, gnawed bones remained.

And the fighting had started again.

Much of the inner city was a skeleton, its bones baked to a brittle white in a thousand fires, some of which still burned. It was a city of roofless, floorless houses and of rutted, pitted roads festooned with fallen cables and choked with debris.

Beirut International Airport was so much concrete

stuck in the midst of faded green. To the east, purple mountains made an eerie backdrop.

They sat down, kissed the runway, and lifted. The wheels went down on the runway again and this time stayed there.

"Necessary bit, that," the pilot said. "Last time I came in here they hadn't cleaned up all the shell craters."

Around the perimeter track, roaring and bumping along to meet the plane as it neared the end of the runway, came an open truck carrying soldiers.

As soon as they turned, the truck slid in front of them. On its back was a sign lettered in French and Arabic, FOLLOW ME.

"I hope you got all them papers you say you got, sir," the pilot quipped.

By the time Carter stepped from the plane it was ringed with hard-eyed, armed Syrian soldiers.

An officer with major's pips on his shoulders met Carter at the foot of the ladder. He was a dark, oily-skinned man with luminous black eyes and a thick mustache. His khaki uniform had accumulated enough salty sweat and grime to stand up by itself.

"Papers."

Carter kept his expression coldly polite and handed them over. The major's thick fingers closed over the documents almost unwillingly. He looked through them grunting, and then back up at Carter with a smirk.

"There is much fighting in the city now."

"I know that."

"You will have to be interviewed by my intelligence superiors before you can be released on your own in Beirut."

"I realize that as well," Carter replied.

One of the soldiers handed him a clipboard. "You will sign this, please."

"What is it?"

"A release. If you, as a foreigner, get kidnapped or killed while in Beirut, it is your own fault. Sign."

"I won't sign," Carter said.

"You will sign or you will get back on the plane."

"I won't sign, Major, because that would give you a chance to shoot me and leave me in a ditch before I ever got into the city."

The major leaned close until Carter could smell his stale breath. "I don't like the *fangii*."

Carter smiled. "That's too bad."

"Of all *fangii*, I hate the French the most, Monsieur Villadame."

"My answer to that, Major, is . . . kiss my ass."

For the briefest of moments, the man's dark face went red. Carter prepared for a blow that never came.

Abruptly, the major whirled on his heel. "You will follow me."

The ride into Beirut was wild. Eight times the soldiers in the back of the truck returned sniper fire.

"Do they know who they are firing at?" Carter asked.

"Anyone who fires at them," was the reply.

Ain't holy war grand? Carter thought.

There was a roughly lettered wooden name plate on the door . . . lettered in Arabic. Carter read it as the major pushed the door open: Colonel Isram Abdallah.

"Inside!" the major said, gesturing.

Carter walked into the room, a large, sparsely furnished office, and the door closed behind him.

He was alone in the room. Alone with his thoughts. Alone to wonder how long the Syrians were likely to delay him here, and how difficult, or how easy, it was going to be to find Leila Samir in the chaos outside that was Beirut.

Restlessly, Carter moved around the big room, taking in the rough desk that slanted across the floor in front of broad windows, the hard-looking, uninviting chairs, and the flatteringly executed portrait of the president of Syria that occupied the place of honor behind and above the desk.

Carter smiled wryly at this. He wondered if a few months ago, or weeks, that place of honor had been occupied by a portrait of Arafat.

Allegiances could change quickly in volatile Lebanon.

Where was Colonel Abdallah?

What was delaying him?

Carter was pretty sure it was just to make him stew.

All right, he thought, *I will stew.*

He took four rapid paces to the door and jerked it open. The corridor beyond was empty, save for a Syrian soldier standing opposite the door as if on guard duty, and who moved his rifle threateningly in Carter's direction as he appeared.

Carter thought it wouldn't be difficult to separate the rifle and the man, but he had to be diplomatic in his dealings with the Syrians. For now, they were in power, and he needed to be able to move around the city with a minimum of hassle if possible.

"Why am I being detained?" Carter demanded in French.

The guard shook his head, not answering, and Carter repeated his question, more loudly, in English. The guard snarled at him then and thrust his rifle forward menacingly.

"I demand to know why I am being kept here!"

Carter barked again in English tinged with a French accent.

"Back!" the guard spat.

And then another voice reached them...a voice speaking carefully controlled English with barely a trace of accent.

A quiet voice. Softly modulated.

"You are being kept here, Monsieur Villadame, for two reasons. One, so that I may interview you to make sure of your reasons for visiting Beirut. Two, I must decide for myself if you are part of yet another Israeli assassination team."

Carter gave no indication, but he knew the man well from his dossier in the AXE files. He was past forty, fairly young for the head of Syrian intelligence, but looked no more than thirty. His face was smooth, utterly unmarked by the tension Carter knew to be there. He was an attractive man, his dark good looks polished by the privileges of birth. From the clear, confident eyes to the manicured nails, he reflected a lifetime of good food, good doctors, good habits and education, all carefully supervised by a procession of strict but adoring nannies, tutors, and assorted servants. He was of moderate height, his shoulders broad and well muscled from regular workouts. His features were blunt but pleasant, his jaw square, his nose slightly snub, the brows that overhung the hazel eyes thick but tamed.

"Colonel Abdallah?"

"Yes." He stopped in front of Carter and eyed him with the same frank curiosity that Carter was extending to him. Then he made a small, almost contemptuous gesture of dismissal and the guard went away.

"Please," he said in that same calm, quiet tone—the voice of a doctor or a priest—"please to step inside." He nodded toward the open door of the office.

Carter went back into the room and sat without being asked. His eyes followed the colonel, whose eyes remained on Carter's. His lean, tanned body moved with a hungry feline grace. Liquid eyes could become hard and flinty. Or they could be totally devoid of any expression. He spoke quietly and with deliberation in flawless French or English as he moved to take his place behind the desk.

"So you are here on behalf of the Jarces Bank in Paris."

"That's correct. We have very large deposits in Euro-Beirut."

Again the colonel flashed him a toothy smile. "Monsieur Julian Daoud's bank."

"That's correct."

"Of course it is."

The man was coy, Carter thought, almost cute. But he was good. It was obvious he knew a great deal more than Reba and the top people at Jarces thought he knew. Carter said nothing.

"And that is all you are here for, Monsieur Villadame?"

Carter paused. It wouldn't pay to play games with this man. He was too sharp. But the Killmaster decided to play one card.

"I would also like to look into the death of Monsieur Daoud. He was a fine man, and my superiors are curious."

"So then you are an investigator as well as an auditor?"

"Not at all," Carter replied. "I, too, am a curious man. Have you caught the murderer yet?"

This brought a bark of laughter. "In Beirut, we call them assassins."

Carter nodded. "Very well. Have you caught the *assassin* yet?"

The eyes turned serious again. "No, Monsieur Villadame, we have not. There are twenty-three different groups currently fighting in Lebanon, including the Israelis now and then. Monsieur Daoud could have been killed by any of them. Do you know the name Hashan Akbar?"

It was an old police trick. Shift gears fast. Catch the subject off-guard. Carter didn't blink.

"No, I am afraid I don't."

"How about Leila Samir?"

Carter felt the tiny muscles in the small of his back near his spine tighten up. Was Abdallah trying to tell him something?

"No, that name means nothing either. Should it?"

Abdallah shrugged. "Probably not. Hashan Akbar was a renegade. He and a group of his friends were wiped out in a house south of the city. It happened about the same time that your Julian Daoud was killed. Of course no one saw anything, except a farmer nearby saw a woman leaving on a motorcycle."

He was trying to say something, Carter thought.

"I'm afraid, Colonel, that it means nothing to me."

"Of course not." Now more than ever Isram Abdallah gave the impression of a man whom only a fool would try to predict or anticipate. "I only mention it to warn you that right now life is cheap in Beirut. Be careful where you go in the city, and how you get there."

"Thank you," Carter said, "I'll do that."

"Where are you staying?"

"My bank owns a flat on the Avenue Ramlet El Baida."

"That wouldn't be the penthouse of number Eighty-one, would it?"

"Yes, it would," Carter said.

"I am afraid that is impossible, monsieur. That is where Monsieur Daoud was killed. It has been sealed for the investigation." Here, Abdallah leaned back in his chair and let his lids droop to hood his eyes. "We find that very strange also."

"Oh?" Carter said, letting his own eyes wander.

"Yes. Daoud's principal residence was a very posh flat on the top floor of the Villa Beirut on the Avenue du Paris. It seems odd that he would transfer his residence for that one night to the Avenue Ramlet El Baida."

"I understand that he was killed with his mistress," Carter said. "Perhaps they wanted new surroundings to rekindle their love life."

"An interesting theory, and, from a Frenchman, quite reasonable." Both men laughed. It had a hollow ring in the room. "But flawed, I'm afraid," the colonel continued. "Daoud brought a bag and his toiletries. His mistress brought nothing. However, her purse was full of money and jewelry, and she wore three pair of panties and two dresses."

Laid out like a map, Carter thought, and the colonel knew it as well. The mistress was running. It was she who betrayed Daoud and set him up for the kill.

"But, monsieur, I detain you too long." He dropped a set of keys in front of Carter. "Since Julian Daoud had no relatives and, according to his will, the Jarces Bank is his executor, I see no reason why you can't avail yourself of his flat on the Avenue du Paris. These are the keys."

"Thank you very much, Colonel," Carter said, knowing full well the reason for the offer.

Colonel Abdallah and his people would have a much easier time of it watching Carter if he were residing in the fishbowl that was the Avenue du Paris.

Abdallah looked at him for another long moment, not speaking. Then he produced Carter's papers and pushed them across the desk. He let his hand lie on them. "As long as you do only what you are accredited to do, no one will have any complaints, monsieur," he said quietly.

And that was all. His hand was removed from the papers. Carter picked them up and nodded. "Thanks."

"I'll have one of my men drive you to Daoud's flat."

"That really isn't . . ."

"Oh, but it is, Monsieur Villadame. Good day."

"Good day, and thank you again."

He had one parting thought as Carter reached the door. "By the way. . ."

"Yes?"

"Please forgive the rudeness of the major who escorted you here. He seems to think your nose rather resembles a goat's penis."

Carter laughed. "It's probably envy, Colonel, from a man who carries only a wart between his legs."

The colonel erupted in genuine laughter. Carter left the office without deciding if the man was going to be a friend or an enemy.

NINE

Villa Beirut was slapped-together-modern, about ten stories high. It and the building on either side of it had avoided most of the carnage of the civil war. Even the street had been cleared of rubble and most of the shell holes repaired.

Carter entered the lobby past a jutting wall of mailboxes to a bank of three elevators. An armed guard stood to one side of the elevators. Evidently the guard had gotten a call from Colonel Abdallah's office. He nodded and pushed the button for Carter.

Inside, Carter pushed the top button and the elevator rose with trembles and groans. It halted on the top floor with a wheeze.

There were two penthouse apartments. The one to the right had Daoud's name on a brass plate.

Out of habit, Carter opened the door of the darkened apartment warily. He reached inside and flicked a light switch that illuminated an entry hall and part of a living room beyond.

Silence.

Satisfied, he entered and closed the door behind him, glancing quickly around.

Julian Daoud had lived well. The living room was tastefully decorated with a sofa, a pair of matching armchairs, and some good modern furniture. Carter walked into the bedroom and wiggled another toggle. A couple of lamps flashed on. He saw a huge brass double bed, a marble-topped bedside table, and another armchair. Everything was covered in expensive materials, a lot of French lace and watered silk.

Carter tossed his bag on the bed and went back into the living room. Bookshelves took up all the space on one wall and were jammed with dozens of leather-bound volumes; tucked into spaces between the books were pieces of pewter, china, and silver. This was no workingman's apartment, Carter thought dryly. It was decorated like a randy millionaire's matinee playpen.

He kicked off his shoes and hit the well-stocked bar. Fortified with a traveling scotch, he did another run through the whole place.

He was sure Abdallah's people had gone through the apartment, but he checked anyway. The two walk-in closets in the bedroom were loaded, his with fine linen and silk suits from Rome and Paris, with a few dark Savile Row pinstripes for business, and hers, the mistress's, equally well stocked. One difference was that all but a very few of the dresses, suits, and skirt-and-sweater sets carried a single label: *Amelia's—Beirut*.

They were expensive clothes, and several of them had that quality and aura that said *original*. Carter made a mental note to check out Amelia's, and walked through the living room to a den-cum-office.

Other than some paper and a few envelopes, the desk had been stripped clean. He removed the drawers, checked under them, and found nothing. Behind a painting of Beirut's main port, there was a safe. It was cracked open and it was empty.

So much for being Daoud's executor, Carter thought. Any papers from the safe would be in Abdallah's office.

Any cash would be in the pockets of his subordinates.

There was a telephone on the desk. He picked it up and, wonder of wonders, it worked. It not only worked, but he was about to dial Paris direct.

"Jarces Paris. May I help you?"

"Yes, Simone Bernstein, please."

"One moment."

Simone Bernstein was the head of the international loan department. She was also heavily involved as a Mossad agent, and the link between the bank in Paris and Reba in London—the only link. Only Simone and one other member of the bank knew of Reba's ownership.

"Oui?"

"Simone, Villadame here. I've landed and am staying in Daoud's flat on the Avenue du Paris."

"Excellent. Will you be going to the bank tomorrow?"

"I will," Carter replied. "By the way, did our people know that Marie Boulard was killed with Julian?"

"It was mentioned, yes."

"The head of intelligence here, a Colonel Abdallah, informed me that the Boulard woman was in our flat on Ramlet El Baida that night by mistake. Out of curiosity, would you check our copy of Daoud's will? I would like to see if she was mentioned."

"I understand. It's almost closing time here in Paris. I'll do it first thing in the morning."

"Thank you. I'll call tomorrow."

Carter hung up. Shortly after he had taken off from London, Reba had flown to Cyprus. She would be contacted there by Paris. If she could feed him any help from there, she would.

Carter checked the phone for a bug. There wasn't one, but that meant nothing. Every phone in the building could be tapped from the main box in the basement, and probably was.

Abdallah would probably figure out the gist of the phone call Carter had just made, but that was all right. Carter wanted him to.

He took off his clothes and headed for the bathroom. The shower was broken. The tub was small, but big enough if he bent his knees. The water was hot. He soaped himself several times and rinsed off with a hand-held spray at the end of a long, snaky metal hose.

Then he lay back and relaxed. He was just figuring the odds against drowning if he took a nap, when he heard an alien sound in the living room.

He sat up abruptly when he recognized the odd buzz as the telephone.

He wrapped a towel around his middle and dashed for the den. He picked it up and held it to his ear without speaking.

After a long pause, a female voice spoke. "Julian? Julian, is that you?"

Carter took a chance. "Leila?" he said, the accent hard on the *e, Lee*-la.

He understood the Arabic word for yes, but not much else of the rapid-fire speech that followed.

He was dead.

His knowledge of the language was rudimentary. If he tried to answer, she would know he wasn't Daoud.

He clicked the phone, grunted, clicked again, and then killed the connection.

With any luck, Leila Samir would think that Julian Daoud was in the apartment. With further luck, she might come to the apartment, since she couldn't get in touch with him by phone.

Obviously she didn't know yet that Daoud was dead.

Carter took thirty seconds to think, then dressed quickly and rushed down to the lobby.

Through a brown dusk heavy with smoke and the smell of burning, Leila Samir moved through the darkening streets.

Around her, this part of the city lay strangely, unnaturally quiet, like a city of the dead.

She had gotten as far north as the Pigeon Rocks. There she had run into two-man Syrian patrols, a dozen of them. She had been forced to turn inland, and now she found herself in a no-man's-land with the Avenue du Paris still far to her left and the fighting Beirut slum areas to her right.

She saw few people, and they were only shapes like herself, moving stealthily in the deep shadows. But, unlike them, Leila moved with a purpose against the backdrop of rubble and debris in the narrow alleys and back streets.

She was still a mile south of Avenue du Paris, directly below the American University. But she was only five blocks from the wide Rue Hamra. There would be no fighting there. That meant that there would be traffic, crowds on the street. Hopefully she could lose herself in those crowds and perhaps find a telephone.

She passed the Commodore Hotel. It was almost rebuilt and the lobby was alive with light. Inside there would be a telephone . . . but there were also Syrian soldiers.

Leila went on. A taxi passed and she resisted the impulse to hold up her hand. Every taxi driver in Beirut was taking money from one group or another to spy and report.

It should have taken her ten minutes to reach Rue Hamra. Because of wandering Amal patrols, barricades, and rubble-blocked streets, it took her nearly an hour.

But once she was there her luck turned. She found a telephone that worked outside an open café. She dialed the number from memory. It rang and rang. She was about to hang up, when it was answered.

But no one spoke.

"Julian? Julian, is that you?"

"Leila?"

"Yes, it's me. Hashan is dead, Julian, if you don't know it already. I have the information. I'll be there in an hour—"

The phone went haywire. It clicked and she could hear Julian trying to speak to her. Then it went dead.

"Damn," she hissed, slamming it back on the cradle.

But at least, she thought, he was there.

She set off again, this time with the hope that she could relieve herself of the responsibility of the knowledge she held, giving quickness to her steps.

Carter lingered in the lobby as long as he dared. When it appeared that the guard was about to question him, he went out to the street and looked around.

He spotted them at once, two teams. One man parked just down the block in a dark Renault. Two men on foot, one pretending to use a phone, the other at an outside table of the café across the street.

Even in civilian clothing, Carter could see and sense their military bearing. When the time came he knew it would be easy to lose them.

For now, he crossed the street, moved through the outside tables and on into the restaurant.

It seemed empty at first because the lighting was dim, but when his eyes became accustomed to the gloom, he could see about a dozen people in the twin, adjoining dining rooms. The maître d', a young man with hair almost to his shoulders and wearing a dinner jacket and black tie above a white apron, came toward him.

"Dinner, monsieur?"

"Oui."

"Follow me, please."

He headed toward the bowels of the restaurant and Carter grabbed his arm. "I'd like a window table, please," he said, pressing an American twenty into the man's hand.

"Of course, monsieur. This way."

He led Carter to a table for two set against a wall, unobtrusive in the elegant surroundings, but with a clear view of the entrance to the Villa Beirut. He pulled a chair out and Carter sat.

"You are alone, monsieur?" he asked.

"Maybe I'll get lucky later," Carter replied dryly.

The maître d' bowed and handed Carter a wine list. When he was gone, Carter scanned the brochure of the contents of the cellar, which was bound in heavy, decorated leather. He noted that the supplies in the basement appeared to be in good order, and the prices respectably outrageous. The maître d' seemed to sense that Carter had made some sort of decision and he came back to hover.

"Has monsieur made a selection?"

"I'll tell you what," Carter said. "Just bring me something simple of your choice. Nothing daring or overly sentimental. And make it red."

"I understand, monsieur." He took the leather folder and left.

The Killmaster lit a cigarette, glued his eyes to the entrance of the Villa Beirut, and sat back to wait.

Under the table, he crossed his fingers.

• • •

Leila Samir approached the building from the ocean side. Once, long ago, she and Hashan had entered this way at Daoud's instructions.

It was black and quiet. She scurried over the promenade and scaled the wall. Shrubbery around the pool hid her from view until she reached the rear entrance.

The door was unlocked. A single flight of stairs led down to the underground garage. Another flight went up. She passed the door marked Elevators, and kept climbing.

The higher she went, the more a musty smell invaded her nostrils. The stairs were evidently rarely used.

At the top floor she made sure the Beretta was loose in the waistband of her skirt under the shawl. Then she pushed through the door.

A dim bulb barely illuminated the small hallway. The elevator indicator told her that the number two car, the only one that went to the top floor, was in the lobby.

She moved to Daoud's door and rang the bell. When there was no answer, she rang again. When still there was no reply, she rapped sharply on the wood.

It was then that she glanced down and saw the edge of a folded slip of paper protruding no more than an inch under the door.

She was about to bend and retrieve it, when every muscle in her body tensed at a sound behind her. She whirled, her fingers on the butt of the Beretta under her shawl.

The door across the hall was open a foot. She could see an elderly man. He was dressed in a silk smoking jacket and he could be anywhere from seventy to ninety.

"What do you want?" He spoke in French with no accent.

Leila answered in the same language. "Please, monsieur, my name is Zena. I am Monsieur Daoud's new maid. I was supposed to meet him here, but when I knocked there was no answer."

The door opened wider, letting the light from the apartment drift into the hall. The man's head was narrow, his face long, and his hair sparse and slicked down close to his skull.

"You are looking for Julian Daoud?"

"Yes."

The man sneered. When he spoke it was almost a snarl. "Where have you been, girl?"

"I . . . I've been in the south . . . one of the camps. Why?"

"Julian Daoud is dead, girl. He was murdered along with his whore. It was in the morning edition of *Annahar*. Don't you read? Go away."

The door slammed.

Leila Samir stood in partial shock, her back to the wall. In her mind she tried to sort it all out and decide on her next move.

Julian was dead. Probably the Israelis.

She would have to get the information to Saif herself. But how? She had no way to contact him. For security reasons, everything had been done through Julian.

Yushi Nuhr. Yes, perhaps she could find Rabani Saif through Yushi Nuhr. But the boutique would be closed at this hour. Did she dare move around in the daytime? Were the Syrians looking for her?

Or, worse yet, the Israelis?

And then she remembered the telephone call. A man had answered and grunted her name. *Who?*

She glanced down at the note. She drew the Beretta, trained it on the door, and snatched the paper free.

She waited a full minute. When the door didn't open, she opened the note. It was in French, a scrawled hand:

Leila,

An important meeting at the Café du Mer across the
street. Have me paged there when you arrive. The
number is 884-112. The door is unlocked.

                                        Julian

Gently she turned the knob and opened the door.
Leading with the Beretta, she entered the apartment.

The meal was, as the French say, *extraordinaire*.
Poached salmon, veal in a cream sauce laced with a
gentle wine and black mushrooms, salad, fresh straw-
berries, and coffee.

Unfortunately, Carter had been able to eat only a few
bites of it. His own watchdogs had been joined now by
at least ten other men. They ranged up and down the
street, and two of them had entered the Villa Beirut.
Obviously since he couldn't see them in the lobby, they
had hidden themselves in the room used by the guards
for breaks.

There was little doubt now that Daoud's phone was
tapped. Carter had not been able to understand the Arabic spoken by Leila Samir. Colonel Abdallah's men
had.

So, he thought, *the Syrians know about the Jordan
Plan*. But *do they know what Leila Samir's current part
in it is*? Even Carter didn't know for sure. It was only
assumption on Tel Aviv's part that Leila knew the location of the missiles.

And perhaps Abdallah was just searching for Leila
because she was there during the Israeli raid and could
point a finger.

In any event, he thought, it looked as though everything was pointless. It had nearly been two hours since
the phone call, and the only female to enter the Villa

Beirut in that time had been at least sixty and two hundred pounds.

He dropped more than enough money for the check on the table, and headed for the door. Halfway to the door he heard the low voice of the waiter moving from table to table.

"Julian Daoud," the waiter was saying in a low voice to match the mood of the restaurant, "telephone call for Monsieur Julian Daoud."

Carter moved quickly through the door and slowed his pace on the street. Calmly he lit a cigarette as he went into the lobby.

TEN

Rabani Saif was fuming. Twenty-four hours and no one had seen her. It was impossible. He had eyes and ears all over the city. If she was moving at all, someone was bound to see her.

Now his informants had told him that the Syrians were also looking for her. And their manpower could move in the open.

They were probably looking for him as well. That was why Saif had come to seek aid from the German, Dieter Bruns.

The man was a bad East German spy who passed himself off as a correspondent in Damascus. Because he had strong connections with the government in Damascus, he was allowed to work in Beirut. Because he knew who to buy in the police and the military, he knew every move the Syrians and the Lebanese police made.

For the right sum of money, Bruns sold Saif anything he wanted to know.

Bruns was a thoroughly dislikable man who had let alcohol get the better of him and had begun drinking at all hours of the day. He was already drunk when Saif arrived that evening. He found him amid a clutter of empty bottles and dirty dishes and cigarette ashes. Saif would not ordinarily have come to Bruns's apartment, but the man had failed to show up at an appointed meeting place. When Bruns heard the patterned knock on the door, he merely yelled from the chair, holding a drink in his hand.

Saif opened the door of the place and entered carefully. He saw Bruns then, across the room with the drink. He closed the door behind him, and locked it.

"Well?" Saif growled.

"You shouldn't have come here," Bruns said, wiping the sweat from his forehead.

"You were to meet me. You never showed." Saif moved to the chair and leaned close to the other man, his eyes glittering. "What important information did you have for me?"

"N-Nothing. It was a mistake," Bruns stammered nervously.

"You lie, Bruns."

"No, I swear—"

Saif knocked the glass from his grasp in a quick movement. The glass shattered on the floor. Bruns came up from the chair awkwardly, his face a dark crimson.

"Damn!" he yelled. He took a swing at Saif.

The Arab avoided the fist and threw a short punch into the man's whiskey-flab belly. The air hissed from his lungs. Bruns staggered, gasping for breath.

Saif hit him again, flush in the face with the heel of his hand. The German crashed over a coffee table and landed hard on the floor, cracking his head.

"Enough!" he moaned. "*Mein Gott*, enough!"

Saif kicked him hard in the side. Bruns cried out in pain and grabbed at his ribs.

"Please . . ." he gasped.

Said hooked a chair with his foot, pulled it near

Bruns, and straddled it. He grabbed the man's hair and turned him over.

"I must find this woman, Bruns. I have to find her, and soon. My people can't locate her. You said the Syrians had a line on her. Now, what do they have!"

"Rabani, please, I can't tell you. If I do, they will know it was me."

"Never. How could they know?"

"I can't . . ."

Saif took a Russian-made automatic from under his shirt. He gripped Bruns's jaw with his left hand until it was open wide. Then he ground the barrel of the gun into his throat.

"I am desperate, Dieter. The Syrians have bought ten times the informers I have in the city. I don't have much time left. If they have found her, I want to get to her first."

Bruns's eyes were wide with fear. He had seen this steel-eyed Arab kill in the past. He knew the man was slightly mad. But he also knew the Syrians. He knew what they could do in their cellars.

He whined and gagged. Saif removed the gun from his throat.

"Talk, Dieter, and I will pay you. Remain silent and I will kill you. It's as simple as that."

The German's fat body quivered. He was between the devil and hell, and he knew it. He could read his own obituary in Saif's eyes.

"She made it to Julian Daoud's apartment on the Avenue du Paris. She is there now, with a Frenchman named Villadame. He is an Israeli spy. The Syrians have the building surrounded. They are going to wait for the Israeli to kill her, and then arrest him."

Saif cursed and stood. Bruns's voice stopped him at

the door. "Saif, they will know it came from me. I will have to leave the city. My money?"

The Arab took a handful of notes from his jacket pocket and threw them in the German's lap.

Bruns's trained eye scanned them quickly and he spat. "That's all? That is all you give me to kill my own fatted calf? This is all you pay me to save your precious Jordan Plan? *Mein Gott*, man, I—"

Saif froze in mid-stride.

Bruns's mouth gaped open. He knew he had said too much.

"How do you know of the Jordan Plan, Dieter?"

"I . . . I don't. I only heard—"

The silencer on the end of the Makarov cracked down, breaking the German's left collarbone. He screamed in pain and Saif lifted his arm again.

"*How*, Dieter? How did you know about the Jordan Plan, and how did you know about the woman being a part of it?"

"Th-the Syrians," Bruns stammered. "I learned it from the Syrians."

"And whom did you tell?"

"No one, I swear!"

"Daoud knew about the Jordan Plan, Dieter. He was an Israeli spy. But he didn't know the location of the safe houses. The Syrians did. They have always known, but as long as we did nothing in their territory, they left us alone."

"Saif, I swear . . ."

The pistol dropped on the other collarbone and Saif's boot slammed into the German's crotch.

"The Syrian, Abdallah, told you, didn't he, Dieter?"

"No, no . . ."

"And you passed it on to the Israelis through Daoud."

Bruns was about to make another denial. He never got the chance.

Saif shot him twice in the center of the forehead.

Carter opened the door slowly with his right hand on the knob. He kept his left arm in the air. He heard no sound, not even breathing.

Before leaving, he had turned on all the lights in the apartment. Now all of them were off except one lamp. It had been tilted to act as a spotlight on the door.

Keeping his hands in sight, he stepped into the hallway, then closed and locked the door behind him.

"Leila Samir?"

"Take four steps forward." Her voice was even, controlled.

He did as he was told. "You know about Daoud, that he's dead?"

"I do now. Turn around. Drop your jacket off your shoulders."

He did, and felt a loop, probably a pull from one of the drapes, cinch the jacket tightly around his forearms.

"Back up slowly."

"Are we going to talk or are you going to just shoot me?"

"Shut up."

She yanked on the line and Carter backed up. Near the center of the room, he heard a chair groan as she stepped on it. He could have taken her then, but he gambled that he could reason better with her if he let her have the upper hand for the moment.

His arms were yanked up painfully behind him. In

turn, his whole body was lifted until he was on the balls of his feet.

The lady, he thought, *is no slouch. She's cool, nervy, and well trained.*

The line was tied off to the chandelier, and she jumped off the chair. The lights came on and she stood in front of him, a Beretta automatic leveled at his gut. His shoulder rig holding the Luger dangled from her left shoulder. He had left it in the false bottom of his bag.

He had seen only a snapshot of Leila Samir, and she looked nothing like that now. Her hair was a mass of tangles, her clothes were filthy and ill-fitting, and grime covered her face.

"Who are you?" she spat.

He had already decided how to play it. "I'm an agent. My name is Carter. Nick Carter."

"Israeli?"

"American."

She shrugged. "Same thing."

"Not quite. Being American, I'm slightly more neutral. My arms are starting to hurt like hell."

"Too bad."

"Look, lady, if I wanted you dead, you'd be dead. I want to talk."

"What about?"

"The Jordan Plan, the two missiles, and your insane friends."

This jarred her a little, but she covered it well. "What happened to Julian?"

"He was killed," Carter said.

"I know that. By whom?"

"I don't know."

"The Israelis," she hissed.

"No," he said. "Of that, I'm sure."

She smiled grimly and edged a little closer, but to the

side so that Carter couldn't use his feet. The Beretta stayed steady in her hand.

"You're sure because you're working with the Israelis."

Carter carefully weighed his words. "In a way, that's true. But if I were totally their man, I would simply kill you so you couldn't pass on the information you have. Tel Aviv would then have all the time in the world to find the missiles and disarm them."

She looked at him almost incredulously for a moment, and then uttered a short, sharp, explosive bark of laughter. "I don't think you're in a position to kill anyone."

Carter did his best to shrug. "Then the Syrians will do it. They know you're in here, and they have the building surrounded."

This brought a spark of fire to her eyes. He continued before she could put it together.

"They are also looking for Rabani Saif. I would imagine that somewhere in Beirut there is also an Israeli hit team looking for him. The chances are good that they will find him before you do."

She dropped wearily into a chair. The Beretta sagged slightly, but not so much that it couldn't be brought back into play quickly.

"What happened?" she asked.

"Daoud worked for the Mossad. He has from the beginning. He tipped the Israelis about the plan. Two teams came into Lebanon by boat off a freighter."

Her mouth turned down in a bitter smile. "I knew about one of them."

"The second team hit Saif's headquarters. They got his copy of the plan, but they missed him."

Her head came up, the dark eyes flashing hatred. "And you're here to stop me from getting to Saif."

"That's right. But I'm doing it my own way."

"Which is . . .?"

"To convince you that the plan was insanity from the first. What could it accomplish? The Israelis won't back down. If the missiles are fired, they will only retaliate. All Saif can accomplish now is to blow up the Middle East. That's not going to get a Palestinian homeland."

He could see in her eyes that he wasn't planting any new seeds. She had already been thinking about what he was saying.

She sensed that he knew, and averted her eyes. "It's war," she said, rising and moving to the bar. "Anything can be condoned in war." She found a soft drink and poured it into a glass, still refusing to meet Carter's eyes.

"Leila, time is running out for you. Everyone is against you. Colonel Abdallah is out there. Why he isn't in here right now, I don't know. It could be that he wants me to do his dirty work for him."

She stared at him for a long moment. "What would you do if I told you where the missiles are?"

Carter spoke slowly, again weighing his words carefully. He had to watch what he said to this woman. Only she knew where the missiles were. If he rubbed her the wrong way, if he antagonized her, then the chance of defusing them would vanish. His mission would have been a total failure. At all costs he must keep her sweet, must reason with her. The success of his assignment depended on his being able to persuade her that it was in her own long-term interests that the Jordan Plan be wiped out of existence, as if it had never been conceived.

"First, I would defuse them. Once that was done, I would blow them up where they are. Without the missiles, Israel can't really prove that the plan was anything more than an idea on paper. Tel Aviv can't embarrass the Syrians or the Palestinians by screaming to the world about Arab insanity."

"Saif and Aman Yassar would simply start over again," she murmured. "They are determined men."

Now, Carter thought, came the tricky part.

"General Yassar is dead. He was assassinated outside Damascus."

Her lip curled. "The Jews are thorough, aren't they?"

"That's why they have survived," he replied. "Well?"

"What about Rabani Saif?"

He remained silent, forcing her to look his way, to meet his eyes. Only then did he speak.

"I've got to kill him."

"You're mad!" she gasped. "You actually want me to help you kill a fellow Palestinian?"

"If you don't, Leila, a great many Palestinians are going to die."

She slumped into a chair. The Beretta dropped into her lap and she began worrying her temples with the tips of her fingers.

Five agonizing minutes passed. It took everything Carter had to remain silent. Finally she came back to life.

"How do we get past the Syrians?" she said calmly.

Carter sighed in open relief. "Take this damn line off my arms and I'll tell you."

ELEVEN

"Well?"

She posed in the doorway. The transformation was astounding. A shower had removed the grime. Carter had chosen the clothes himself from Marie Boulard's closet. Leila was taller and a size larger than Daoud's mistress, but that might work to their advantage. The way the azure-blue silk blouse and white linen slacks fit, any man would be hard pressed to study her face.

His eyes fell on her chest. "Bra?"

Her face flushed slightly. "None of them would fit."

"Then find a sweater or jacket. That's all a little too much. And make a turban out of some scarves for your hair."

She was back in two minutes.

"Better, much better. But for now, leave the jacket open. The old man may be past seventy, but he's still alive."

He checked the note she had written one last time:

Julian,
It wasn't safe to wait here for you. I will meet you in the lobby of the Alexander Hotel at 10:00 tomorrow morning.

Leila

Carter crumpled the paper and tossed it into a waste-basket.

"Do you think the Syrian colonel will buy that?"

"I think he will, for a while," Carter replied. "C'mon, let's give the little Frenchman across the hall a thrill."

They moved into the hall. Carter locked the door of Daoud's apartment. Leila was already at the other door. Carter pointed to the brass plaque—HENRI ROUILLAC—and moved to the side of the door.

She nodded and rang the bell. It was nearly a full minute before the door opened a crack.

"Pardon, Monsieur Rouillac?"

"Yes, what is it?"

"I am from UNESCO, monsieur. I know it is late, but we have been asked to poll all French citizens still in Beirut . . ."

"I don't know . . ."

Leila charged on, her heavy breasts practically jutting into the crack in the door. "You are French, are you not, monsieur?"

"Yes, but . . ."

"I would just like to talk to you for a few moments . . ."

The door closed. Leila nodded. Carter could hear the chain being removed. It was open again only an inch when he pushed his shoulder to it.

The little man cried out in alarm, but he was powerless against Carter's rush. Before he knew it, he had been forced back into his living room and unceremoniously dumped on his own sofa.

"Monsieur Rouillac, we are two very desperate people. We need your help to get out of the country. If you do exactly as we say, you will come to no harm. Do you understand?"

The little man's face was white and he was gasping for breath.

Leila saw the signs and shoved his head between his knees. At the same time, she put her lips close to his ear and spoke in a low, soothing, almost sultry voice.

"Be calm, monsieur, take even breaths. You are going to be fine. Just relax. We mean you no harm."

On and on it went until his breathing was even and the color had returned to his cheeks. Then Leila gently stretched him out on the sofa and tenderly patted his face.

"Everything is going to be fine, monsieur. Are you alone here?"

"I am alone," he rasped, nodding weakly.

"Are you feeling all right now?"

"Y-yes."

"Good, good," she cooed, and joined Carter at the door.

"Can you handle him?" the Killmaster murmured.

She nodded. "He will be entertained until the time comes."

"You've got the number?"

"Yes," she said. "Let it ring three times and hang up . . . let it ring twice and hang up."

"Right. Don't call until you're sure they have searched Daoud's apartment and left."

"Abdallah will leave men in the lobby or on the street."

Carter smiled. "That's what the old man's for, remember?"

The Killmaster memorized the Frenchman's telephone number and slipped through the door. He waited until he heard the chain slip into place, and then headed for the elevator.

• • •

Outside, he created minor chaos among the watchers. He could tell from the movement that their orders didn't include instructions on what to do if he came out alone.

One man in a radio car was desperately trying to hide a hand mike with a newspaper. Carter turned left on the Avenue du Paris and set a brisk pace. There were two walkers behind him and one man, in the Renault, sped half a block in front and slowed, pacing him.

At the Phoenicia Inter-Continental Hotel, Carter mounted the steps and entered the lobby. The Phoenicia was one of the hardest hit by Israeli shells and phosphorous bombs. But now, even though the top floors were closed, the rubble had been cleared away and part of the hotel reopened.

It was a little past midnight. In the distance to the south, the shelling could be heard. But the huge hotel lounge was open and doing a raging business.

Carter noticed that his shadow had moved into the lobby and taken up a position by the door.

At the bar, Carter ordered a drink and kept his eyes on the front entrance. Number Two walker was probably in the rear of the hotel somewhere, he thought, which told him what he wanted to know.

He finished the drink, went back out into the lobby, and approached the desk.

"Monsieur?"

"Yes, I know it's late, but I have to leave early in the morning. I wonder if I might be able to change some money?" As he spoke, Carter slid his hand across the counter. When he lifted it, he left two twenty-dollar bills on the highly polished wood.

The grin was tight-lipped but wide. "I think that can be taken care of, monsieur. Would you step over here to the cashier's cage, please?"

Carter moved around the counter. His tail was still by

the door, looking foolish behind his newspaper. The cashier's area, Carter was glad to see, was out of the man's view.

"Dollars into Beirut pounds, monsieur?"

"No. As a matter of fact, I'm going to Italy. I wonder if you have lire, cash, small bills... about three hundred dollars' worth, please?"

The man chuckled. "Monsieur, three hundred dollars' worth of small lire? Do you have a suitcase, monsieur?"

Carter himself laughed. "I want to feel like I'm rich," he replied.

The man shrugged and began counting out the bills. It took nearly twenty minutes, and Carter's pockets were stuffed with money when he returned to the street.

He walked the ten or so blocks south to Rue Hamra. It was bustling with a lot of people moving both ways. Now and then the eddies of humanity would clot up at a stoplight, blocking all traffic until they separated again.

He turned left and strolled casually along, making sure that his two walkers were close behind. Abdallah's man in the sedan was hopelessly bottled up in traffic blocks behind.

Farther south, the sound of exploding rockets and mortars had subsided slightly. Probably on a midnight-snack break, Carter thought wryly, spotting a likely-looking café.

He entered, ordered a drink, and waited. Three minutes later, one of the walkers came in and took a table in the rear. The other took up a position on the sidewalk.

When he saw the sedan finally catch up and park across the street, Carter moved, fast.

Outside, he turned back toward the west and ran. His watchers were thrown off for a full minute. The man in the sedan was caught flatfooted. He couldn't get the car turned anywhere near fast enough.

At a light, with about a block between himself and his pursuers, Carter broke through an extra heavy knot of people. On the other side, he stopped and began shouting in French. At the same time, he threw great wads of money high into the air. The bills flew from his hands and fluttered back down to the pavement and the crowd.

In seconds the street and sidewalks in both directions turned chaotic. Men, women, and children scrambled for the bills.

By the time his two running pursuers hit the wall of humanity, Carter was down a side street. He zigzagged his way through several streets until he reached the area around the old parliament building.

"Monsieur?" the driver inquired as Carter ducked into a cruising taxi.

"East," Carter replied, "anywhere along the Avenue Charles Helou."

Reba's backup contact in Beirut was Dr. Renée Saisse. She had her offices and living quarters in a large old villa in the hills just outside the city's eastern boundary.

It would still be a twenty-minute jog after he left the cab, but worth it. Finding his route would be impossible once he left the cab.

Carter rang the bell and the door was opened by a maid wearing a white cap and a tiny scrap of apron over a black dress.

"Oui?"

"I must see Dr. Saisse."

"The office is closed, monsieur. It is almost one—"

"I am aware of that. This is an emergency. I am one of her old patients."

"Your name, monsieur?"

"Villadame, Nicolas Villadame. I am sure she will see me."

The maid widened the door for him to enter, and with a sweet smile and a tantalizing rustle of taffeta showed him into the foyer.

"Un moment, s'il vous plaît."

"Oui."

She went away.

Carter looked around the room. If one liked modern art, the cream of it was displayed on the walls. There was the heavy-handed vigor of Roualt, the giraffe-necked women of Modigliani, and the linoleum designs of Mondrian. All these valuable paintings floated above a sea of antique Oriental carpets.

The room and what Carter could see beyond it was expensive. The rest of Beirut might have been blown up—or currently be blowing up—but Dr. Renée Saisse was weathering it quite well.

He was kept waiting long enough to ensure that he was suitably impressed before there came a gentle knock on the door and a platinum blonde entered.

She looked as if she might be gold-plated and diamond-studded. She was tall and statuesque, detachedly beautiful and with a great figure. She spoke perfect French with only a slight but very charming accent, and wore a severely cut black dress with a hobble skirt that emphasized her rounded femininity. She was as remote as a star, and acknowledged Carter with an impersonal "Good evening." As she did so, she exuded an aromatic fragrance that made him acutely aware of the freshness of her skin. "Monsieur Villadame?"

"Yes. Forgive the hour, Doctor, but I find myself in need of your services at once."

"This way, please."

Her study was more artwork and glove-soft leather furniture.

She gestured Carter toward a spindly-legged, valuable antique chair, crossed to a writing desk of the same period, and seated herself facing him. On the desk before her was an enormous ornate, leather-bound ledger. She opened it.

From the ledger she took half of a five-hundred-franc bill and slid it across the desk. Carter twisted the heel of his right shoe, produced the other half of the bill, and matched the edges.

"I thought you would contact me sooner."

"Things have been happening," he replied dryly.

"I have only two absolutely trustworthy people," she said, frowning. "I am afraid we have come up with very little on the woman that will help you."

Carter jiggled his hand. "No matter. I have her."

The frown turned into a smile. "You are even better than Paris said you would be."

"Luck, a lot of it," he said. "Right now I need some makeup to darken my skin, and a jacket and cap, as close to what cab drivers wear as possible."

"That is no problem. What else?"

"A taxi."

She didn't even blink. Carter told her the whole tale, and how he planned on getting Leila Samir out of the hotel.

When he finished, she stood. "There is liquor in the corner cabinet. I will be back in a few moments."

Carter helped himself to a brandy. She was back in ten minutes.

"Sit here. I will do your face. I thought a mustache would also help."

"Good idea," he said, slipping out of his jacket and taking the chair. "Is Cyprus in place?"

"Yes. I was in contact just an hour ago. They have everything ready. There is a boat, the *Norivadad*, in the private boat area of the port."

"Near the crossing?" he asked.

"Yes, Pier Four. The captain's name is Abbas Tomal. He will take you to a freighter lying out about fifteen miles. Everything you need is in that briefcase on my desk."

In fifteen minutes Carter couldn't recognize himself.

The telephone on her desk did its thing. Both of them stood, transfixed, waiting. It rang three times and stopped. Then it rang two times and went silent.

"That's it," Carter growled.

He dialed, and Leila picked it up on the first ring.

"How goes it?"

"They have been gone about twenty minutes," she replied. "I don't think they left anyone in the apartment."

"Good," he replied. "Is the old man dressed and ready?"

"Yes."

"Does he know what to do?"

"He has agreed to cooperate. I have assured him that we will let him go in a matter of blocks."

"All right. Hit the lobby doors in exactly thirty minutes. Act like you own the town. Walk the service drive to the Avenue du Paris. I'll be across the street headed east in front of the restaurant."

"The car?" she asked.

Carter held his hand over the mouthpiece and turned to Dr. Saisse. "The taxi?"

"A dull red, large dent in the left rear fender," she replied. "A Renault Twelve. No checker stripe."

The lack of a checker stripe meant the cab and driver had a security clearance and could go to the airport and port areas.

Carter repeated it all to Leila. She got the inference. "We are going to the airport?"

"No," he replied. "Thirty minutes."

He hung up and shrugged back into his shoulder rig. Over this he pulled on a dark leather jacket.

He checked the mechanism of the Luger, made sure the clip was full, and slipped it back into the holster. He took three spare clips from the briefcase and slipped those into his pockets.

"Passports and beeper?" he said.

The woman inserted the tip of a crimson fingernail into the seam of two leather strips that formed a partition in the briefcase, and drew them apart. She withdrew two passports and a tiny transmitting bug.

Carter placed the bug in the heel of his right shoe. "How long is it good for?"

"Twenty-four hours."

He nodded. The little transmitter would be his calling card so the men on the freighter would not waste time asking questions but get them right aboard and on their way.

He examined the passports they would need to get through the Syrian patrols at the port. They were convincingly aged and half-full of good foreign visas, as well as showing an entry stamp into Beirut dated two weeks before. They contained fuzzy photos of Carter and Leila, and listed the names Thomas Lodge and Fatima Lodge. Thomas had been born in London, Fatima in Cairo.

Tucked in her passport was a well-creased marriage

certificate issued by a London registrar's office some years ago.

"Good, very good," Carter offered.

"I have a tracking device and screen upstairs in my quarters," Dr. Saisse said. "As soon as you are at sea, I'll contact Cyprus."

"Thanks for your help," he said.

She smiled. "Let's hope I see no more of you."

"I'll second that," Carter growled, and headed for the street and the taxi.

TWELVE

The traffic had thinned out, both cars and pedestrians, but there was still enough so that no single car nor a walking couple would draw undue attention.

Carter stopped the Renault a block from the restaurant. He lit a cigarette and let it dangle from the corner of his mouth. The bill of his cap was pulled low. From beneath it he studied the wide glass doors of the Villa Beirut and the street between himself and the restaurant.

He knew Colonel Abdallah's men were there, but he couldn't spot them.

He checked his watch: two minutes to go.

A thin little mouse of a woman in a shapeless black dress, black stockings, and low-heeled shoes poked her head through the passenger window.

Her voice was reed-thin. Carter shrugged. He couldn't understand a word she said.

She spoke again, waving her hands, and reached for the rear-door handle. Quickly, Carter reached across the seat and locked the door.

Again she leaned through the window and began to berate him.

Carter resorted to French. "I am on hire for the night, a rich *fangii* . . . get on, you bag of bones."

She cursed him roundly but moved on down the street.

Ten seconds.

He dropped the Renault into first gear and eased slowly forward.

The little Frenchman and Leila Samir were just emerging from the apartment house. The man looked nervous but he was holding up. Leila was playing her part well, shoulders back, head up, her eyes straight forward.

Their feet had scarcely hit the curb when Carter halted the taxi right beside them. He leaned across the seat and pulled up the door lock. Leila pushed the Frenchman into the back seat and followed him.

Carter dropped the flag on the meter and moved.

"Spot them?" he asked.

"Yes," Leila replied, "two in the lobby. I don't think they paid any attention to us. How about the street?"

Carter shrugged. "If they were there, I didn't see them."

He turned right at the first big street, went half a block, and turned into the parking lot of the Holiday Inn. He kept going to the far rear of the hotel and pulled up at the trash dumpster.

In one movement he was out of the car and had the rear door open. "Out!"

The Frenchman didn't move. Sweat poured from his face. Leila pushed and Carter pulled. The man stumbled from the car right into a sitting position with his back against the dumpster.

"Sit there for fifteen minutes. Don't move, don't shout, and you'll be fine. Understand?"

A weak nod.

Carter dived back into the driver's seat and hit the street. He went on south to Rue Bliss, and turned east again. He followed this until he passed the old Green Line that had once separated East and West Beirut, all the time checking the mirror.

At the Place des Martyrs, he took the traffic circle and started to turn north again toward Avenue du Paris.

He never made it. A Fiat got inside and cut him off, forcing him to continue east. It was impossible to tell if it was done on purpose or not when it happened.

Two blocks farther on, Carter knew for certain. The Fiat continued around the circle and came on. A block farther on, it was joined by a Big Citroën sedan.

Leila spoke for the first time since they had dumped the Frenchman. "What is it?"

"Can't tell yet, two cars. But if they're after us, it must be Abdallah's people."

She climbed over into the front seat. "How can we be sure?" she asked, turning around to watch their rear.

"Only one way," Carter murmured, flooring the Renault and not getting much of a result.

The Citroën sailed around the smaller car and came on fast. The Fiat peeled off. Carter guessed the smaller car would get ahead of them on a parallel street and try a cutoff.

He kept his foot on the floor. The car bucked and swayed, scraping across potholes. An oncoming bus whipped toward them. Carter used it to hold off the Citroën who was trying to come up alongside.

"We've passed the port area," Leila said.

"I know," Carter muttered, and then glanced her way. "Who said we were heading for the port?"

She came right back. "You told me on the phone that we weren't going to the airport."

She was right; he had told her that. Anyway, he didn't have time to think about it now.

They were on the open road now, climbing into the

hills away from the sea. The rearview mirror held nothing but darkness, but he was pretty sure the Citroën was still back there. And the road he was on would eventually angle back to the sea and the corniche.

Ten to one, he thought, *that's where the Fiat is waiting.*

The road wound through shacks and shanties, a colorless blur at this hour. After about five minutes on a straight road, he flashed another glance in the mirror. This time twin lights flickered back there. He rounded a curve, the car whipping sideways, then at the next flat run he looked again: lights dipped below a hill, reappeared, coming fast.

He took a tight bend without braking, fighting the wheel while the tires fought the road for possession. Then an uphill curve and he went into it in a racing turn, swinging wide, and trusting to luck that no one was coming out. Now, stretching before his high beams what looked like a straightaway . . . but for how far? The Citroën behind was closing in.

At the next curve Carter gained distance, shrieking downgrade, but he couldn't go any faster. There was no time to look for a side road. The other car was going to overtake, crowd them off the road, or start shooting when it came alongside.

A lot of things happened within the next few seconds. He jammed on the brake so suddenly that he slammed forward against the wheel. The Renault swerved, practically standing on its nose as it bucked to a halt.

But the barreling hulk of the Citroën hurtled by. Dead ahead a blind corner, too close, too soon, too late for the fast-moving car to take . . . veering, swaying out of control.

Carter thought.

But the driver of the Citroën was good, damn good. Somehow he brought it under control. The tires screamed and sparks flew from a fender shearing a metal guardrail, but the big car came to rest sideways across the road.

The Killmaster was all flying hands as he reversed the Renault, stopped, and started back the other way. Over Leila's shoulder he could see men pouring out of the Citroën waving their arms.

Lights were coming up the hill behind them.

"It's the Fiat," Carter hissed. "Hang on, I'm going around him!"

"No!"

Before Carter could stop her, Leila reached over, turned off the engine, and yanked the keys from the ignition.

In gear, the Renault's engine complained for a few feet and then rocked to a halt.

"Damn you!" Carter yelled, and whirled in the seat.

She held the Beretta steady in both hands, the barrel inches from his face.

"Shit," he growled. "Saif?"

She nodded. "I couldn't help you kill—"

He didn't hear the rest of it. Powerful hands were dragging him from the car. When he tried to fight back, a chop to the side of his neck sent him into a well of darkness.

Carter came awake to the sound of harsh voices. Two, perhaps three male voices raised in anger on one side. He recognized Leila Samir's voice on the other side of the argument.

He half-opened one eye. He was on the floorboard of a car, probably the Citroën. Outside the car he could see stars. They were fuzzy, but clear enough to tell him that they were heading south. He could have also guessed from the lack of buildings and the sound of shells exploding and occasional small-arms fire.

For over an hour he floated in and out of consciousness. There was a weight on his chest. When he opened his eyes he saw that it was a man's foot.

He could hear no gunfire now. The car windows were open and sand was blowing in. It burned his face. He coughed and choked on it and someone laughed.

"Hey, Leila, your benefactor is awake!" Eyes leaned over him. The rest of the face and head was hidden by a kaffiyeh. "Ah, *fangii*, it is good you are alive."

Carter moved and another foot kicked the side of his head.

The hell with it, he thought, and let the blackness blanket him again.

The journey on the floor in the back of the car seemed interminable. Time lost its meaning for him and he had no idea of the distance they had traveled when the car finally stopped.

Nor did he wonder what was going to happen to him. He was too consumed by the pain in his head, the aching bruises on his ribs and throughout his whole body to care very much. Occasionally he recognized the voices of the men, and when the car halted he heard another man's voice. But it meant nothing to him and he let himself be carried through a pattern of light and shadow involved with the pain he felt.

The light dissolved from the patterns flickering behind his eyelids and became all darkness. Perhaps he slept. He wasn't sure. He was aware of time moving sluggishly through the heat and darkness that encompassed him. Once, someone came in and poured some water through his clenched teeth. He started to spit it out, then tasted, and drank a little of it. A voice complained querulously about his condition, but he couldn't identify the speaker.

He was left alone for a long time after that, falling in and out of sleep.

When he awakened enough to think rationally, he could smell food. It gagged him.

He was on a cot and when he tried to sit up, he found his wrists and ankles bound to the four corners of the narrow bed. He was unable to raise himself more than two or three inches. It seemed an irrational sort of restraint and he wondered about it.

From what he could see of the room, he was in part of a shack or lean-to with sides. Bright sunlight gleamed through cracks in a worn green shade pulled over the single window.

The door opened and Leila stepped into the room. She had changed into mottled green fatigues. There was a cartridge belt around her hips and a heavy automatic. She carried a thick mug in one hand. The aroma coming from it was strong. Turkish coffee.

"You're awake."

"More or less."

"How do you feel?"

"Like shit. But I'm alive, no thanks to you."

She gazed at him steadily, coolly. "I couldn't let you kill my brothers." She came closer to the cot. "This is coffee. If you give me your word you won't try anything, I'll untie one of your hands so you can drink it."

Carter met her eyes and held them. She was the first to blink and look away.

"Well?"

"Why not?" he said. "I have no plans now anyway."

She set the mug on the floor and untied his left hand. Quickly she backed away as he flexed his wrist and fingers to restore the circulation.

"You called them from the old man's apartment while I got the taxi." It was a statement, not a question.

"Yes. I called the shop of Saif's mistress. Luckily, someone was there to relay my message."

"Great," he growled. "Got a cigarette?"

She lit one and rolled it across the floor. Carter alternated his free hand between the coffee and the cigarette.

"Rabani is going to let you live," she said softly.

"Oh? Why?"

"When we reach the missiles and arm them, you will be taken to the Israeli frontier and released along with our demands."

Carter snorted. "Jesus, Leila, I thought you had some sense. It's over. It was over before it started. Can't you see—"

She stood. "Have you finished the coffee?"

"Yeah. I'm hungry."

"Food will be ready shortly. Return your hand to the bar above your head."

He did. As she reached to bind him, he grasped her wrist in the vise of his fingers. That was all. He didn't yank or twist; he just held her.

"If you let that maniac go on with this, we'll all die," he hissed.

"The Israelis will negotiate . . ."

"Like hell they will!"

"Let go of my wrist."

He did, and she retied his arm to the bar in silence. When she finished, she tested the knot and moved back to the door.

"Leila . . ."

She hesitated, then turned. "Yes?"

"Where are we?"

"Near Rasheiya, at the foot of Jabal Ash Shaykh."

Carter concentrated. "About fifteen miles from the Syrian border."

"That's right. Come nightfall, we will cross over the mountains into Syria and head south. Remember what I said . . . cause no trouble and Saif will let you live."

She closed and locked the door behind her.

Carter looked down at his feet. The beeper in his heel had about twelve hours of life left in it.

He wondered what its range was.

It was hot. Carter dozed. At noon they brought him food, two men, tall, broad and mean-looking with heavy beards and scarred arms.

Once again one arm was freed just long enough to stuff the food in his mouth. Then he was retied and they were gone.

At dusk the door opened again. Rabani Saif himself came into the room. Carter recognized the darkly handsome face instantly. There were over a dozen good shots of the man at AXE headquarters in Washington.

A woman Carter guessed to be Yushi Nuhr—tall, good figure, handsome features—moved in behind Saif. She took up a position by the door, cocked an AK-47, and leveled it at Carter.

Saif came directly to the cot. A knife appeared from beneath the Bedouin robes he wore. With two quick moves he cut the ropes from Carter's wrists. This done, he dropped his tall, powerful body into a crouch directly in front of the Killmaster. He lit two cigarettes and passed one over.

"Beyond what Leila has told us, I do not care. Who you really are, I do not care, so I need not interrogate you."

Carter dragged deeply on the cigarette. "I probably wouldn't tell you anything anyway."

The black eyes glittered as they appraised him openly. "No, you probably wouldn't. And that is as it should be. Leila has told me of your philosophic argument in Daoud's apartment. You sound like a man of reason. I, too, am a man of reason. I am not a Shiite of the Hezbollah. I do not kiss the fingers of the hand that wipes the mullah's ass."

He paused, smoking, as if he were waiting for some kind of reply from Carter. When none came, he took a last deep drag on his cigarette, ground it out beneath his heel, and continued.

"I do not fight for my religion or for leaders who grow fat in another country. I fight for myself and my own pride. I tell you this, Carter, so you will know that I mean to carry out what you know as the Jordan Plan. Do you understand?"

Carter ground out his own cigarette and let his eyes float from Saif to the woman. "You are Yushi Nuhr?"

"I am," she said, nodding.

"Rabani Saif is your man?"

"He is."

"Yushi Nuhr," Carter said evenly, "I don't think you are mad. I think your man is."

Saif chuckled, a low rumble from his broad chest. "She is quite prepared to die, Carter. We all are. You have no allies here."

Carter turned back to the crouched Arab and leaned forward. "You are mad, you know."

The man nodded. "Probably. Quite probably."

He stood and snapped his fingers. A man moved into the room and tossed some robes on the cot.

"We leave right after dusk. You will dress like the rest of us, like a Bedouin. We will be walking over the mountain. We can't tie you because a shepherd or farmer seeing us would think it odd and report it to the

Druse who control this area. Do you understand?"

"Yes."

"If we meet anyone and you try to escape or even shout, you will be dead. Do you understand this?"

"Perfectly," Carter growled.

"Good." Saif laid a hand on Carter's shoulder. "We will succeed, Carter, believe me. Your name might even go down in the history books alongside mine." He turned on his heel and strode from the room.

The woman, Yushi Nuhr, stood for a moment longer staring at Carter. He stood and moved toward her. The rifle didn't bobble, nor did Carter. He moved right into it until the barrel was an inch into his belly.

"He is, you know, quite mad," he said simply.

THIRTEEN

The moon was a sliver and the stars illuminated little as they moved, single file, up the mountain.

Besides Carter, Saif, and the two women, there were four other men. All of them had that world-weary look in their eyes that comes to fighting men when the war has gone on too long. But they were still sharp and alert. Carter quickly surmised that they were also loyal to Saif, probably to the death.

There would be no quarter there.

They passed the low dark bulk of a single farm building, a dog yapping at them until they were far beyond it. After that there were no more buildings, nor even any farms. Before long it became obvious why. The land tilted and became the steep, rocky slopes of a mountainside. Frequently they had to detour around jumbles of boulders and wild groves of trees. Ravines that cut down the side of the mountain forced longer detours. The wind grew colder and stronger, whipping the dark tree shapes around them, yanking at the kaffiyehs and long robes they wore.

In the line, Carter was toward the front, with Yushi Nuhr leading him and Leila Samir at his heels.

Twice in the first hour he lagged back in an attempt to engage Leila in a whispered conversation.

She would have none of it. Her only reply was to prod him with the barrel of the assault rifle hidden beneath her robes.

It was close to midnight when they reached the top of the mountain and Saif called a short rest break.

Carter found himself isolated on a rock, with the others grouped around him in a circle several feet away. They paid very little attention to him, but he knew that if he even made a move to bolt, the night would echo with the clicks of shells being chambered.

He raised his voice. "Am I allowed one of my own cigarettes?"

There was a rumble of voices and some movement. Finally Leila crossed to one of the men and held out her hand. Reluctantly he passed over Carter's lighter and cigarette case.

She moved to where he sat and gave them to him. Carter opened the case, lit two, and handed her one of them. "Join me?"

She looked uncomfortable, but she took the cigarette and sat on a nearby rock.

"After we cross this corner of Syria, how deep do we go into Jordan?"

To his surprise, she answered promptly. "A few miles south of Golan."

Carter measured her. "Have you given the location and the rest of the information to Saif?"

She nodded. "And to Yushi Nuhr as well. If anything happens to one of us, the other two will carry on."

"And if all three of you are taken out?" Carter asked.

She looked at him coolly. "That wouldn't concern you. If that should happen, you will already be dead."

They smoked in silence for a minute. Then Carter leaned forward. "I am a fool, Leila. I should have killed you in Daoud's apartment."

Her only reaction was a slight shrug. "Perhaps you should have."

Saif called to them, and they started the trek down the mountain and into Syria.

The sun was just rising, a bright ball on the horizon, when they reached a track that curved for some distance through two high shelves of rock. On either side were other upthrust wedges of rock, dark slabs, their shape almost wholly hidden by drifts of sand.

Carter sensed the sudden alertness of the others. Two of Saif's men jogged ahead, no longer hiding their guns beneath their robes.

The Killmaster could guess why. Sometime during the past two hours they had crossed the frontier into Syria. At any time they could run into a military patrol.

Then the ground began to level out. They emerged from the rock tunnel. Ahead of them, a string of men squatted on their haunches beside a truck.

They wore a variety of ragged clothes, filthy jackets, stained, baggy trousers, dirty turbans, and worn boots.

Two of them rose and conferred with Saif. He did most of the talking, with them nodding. Eventually all but two of the men disappeared back up the rock tunnel. The two remaining climbed into the cab of the truck.

Leila prodded Carter. "Onto the truck bed, under the canvas."

Carter did as he was told.

There was no hope now, he thought, that the beeper had done any good.

They drove for nearly an hour. Sometimes they were on the semblance of a road. Most times they went directly across the sand.

When they stopped at last and rolled off the truck, Carter spotted what appeared to be a Bedouin camp. At the base of the ruin of an old two-story building, several tents were pitched. There were a few trees around the sand compound, and milling among the tents he could see women and children.

Saif approached him. "I suggest you rest, Carter. The worst of the trip is yet to come."

"No matter where the war or how fiercely it is fought, nothing stops the movement of the Bedouin across the desert sand. For freedom is his right, and no war nor man can stop his flight."

Saif smiled. "Quite right. Out here a caravan always has the right of movement. Whom do you quote?"

"Myself," Carter quipped. "When I'm not killing people I moonlight as a poet."

He was led to a small tent at the side of the ruined building. Inside, he was tied to the center pole by his wrists. His legs they left free.

Alone, he reflected on his position. Saif would use the pretext of a Bedouin caravan to cross the frontier into Jordan. There was a good chance that they would then leave the caravan and head directly to the site of the missiles.

Besides the women and children in the camp, Carter had counted about fifteen men. They were a hard lot, and well armed.

He didn't have to think twice. He would hold off making any move until they left the caravan. Saif and his men would be tough to handle, but the numbers would be better.

At noon, a pretty young girl with delicate features and bronze skin entered the tent with a bowl of food. As she fed him from the bowl, Carter tried conversation in French.

He never knew if she didn't understand or just

wouldn't listen. She never said a word. When the bowl was empty she left.

Carter dozed. It was difficult to sleep sitting upright and tied to a pole, but eventually the weariness of an overnight march over a mountain overcame discomfort.

It was dusk when they came for him, two of them. They marched him into the ruined building.

Saif stood by a table. On the table were two canvas-covered mounds. When Carter was directly in front of Saif by the table, the man peeled down the canvas.

The two mounds were bodies. They were both in their twenties. The djellabas they had been wearing were pulled down to their waists. Bullets had been stitched across their chests in even rows.

"They were Israelis, Carter, commandos. I don't know how they followed us into the mountains from Beirut, but they did. I imagine you know how this was accomplished."

He paused. Carter made no comment.

"In any event, Carter, please remember it is you who is responsible for their deaths."

He turned and barked orders to others in the room. They carried the bodies out for burial.

Outside, the tents had been taken down and packed in a line of motley trucks.

How odd, Carter thought, pushing the picture of the two young dead men from his mind, *trucks have taken the place of camels.*

They drove all night. Once again, most of it was directly over the sand in a zigzag pattern. Carter could only sense when they passed into Jordan. It came from a certain tightness on the faces of those around him.

Their contact, their assurance of a safe passage, General Aman Yassar, was dead. Israeli Mossad would know they were on the move. There was a good chance that Jordanian patrols were looking for them.

Carter said as much to Leila who sat beside him.

"So?" she said with a shrug.

Carter chuckled hollowly. "The Israelis want to stop you, the Jordanians want to stop you, the Syrians would like to see you dead. My God, if Arafat were here, *he* would order you stopped."

"We no longer take orders from anyone," she said icily.

"Leila, every Arab in the Mideast would call this madness. Can't you see that?"

"Israel will negotiate," was her only reply.

When Carter started to speak again she moved to another part of the truck away from him.

Two hours before dawn, the truck in which they were riding left the caravan. Now they were on a road and still heading south.

The countryside began to change. They passed trees and rock-terraced slopes. There were even cultivated fields. It was a fertile valley. That could only mean they were near the Jordan River.

Finally the truck lurched onto a secondary, potholed track and between two gateposts. Minutes later they halted in front of an old stone cottage that probably provided shelter for shepherds or farm workers during the season.

Carter was hustled inside.

It was one large room. At the far end was a large, open fireplace with smoke-blackened walls. The floor was carpeted with dried sheep droppings, and two small windows gave ventilation and enough daylight to show the simple furniture; a solid kitchen table was flanked by two long benches, a mildewed mattress with stuffing leaking from one corner lay on the floor, and there were two wobbly chairs.

One of the men started to build a fire. The others carried supplies in from the truck.

They started to push Carter into a corner. One man produced a rope to tie his arms.

"Wait. I've got to piss."

They kept pushing him, but Saif called out from the other side of the room, "That's all right. Yushi, take him outside. Let him relieve himself."

All the men laughed. It was the ultimate insult, guarded by a woman while he relieved himself.

As Carter stood, watering the pebbled sand with Yushi Nuhr nearby watching his every move, he scanned the surrounding countryside.

It was bleak. Nothing but sand and hills.

Far, far to the west, through the heat haze, he could just make out the valley they had driven through. Somewhere in the middle of that valley would be the river. And just beyond the river was Israel.

He headed back toward the cottage. He had gone only a few steps when he saw something in the sand catch the sun's glare. A few feet farther on he spotted another tiny glint.

He lifted his eyes to the rear wall of the cottage. There was a line of new mortar all the way across the wall. Just above was the shadow of a hairline crack . . . or an opening.

Inside, he allowed himself to be tied and thrust into a corner. When they moved away, he rolled toward the wall. Carefully he scanned the place where the dirt floor met the wall. He spotted a daub of grease on the stone. A few feet away there was another, and then another.

He put it all together. The glints he had seen in the sand were tracks, or rails.

The grease on the stones. The crack or opening above the newly mortared stones in the outside wall.

He was lying right on top of the two missiles.

FOURTEEN

The chartered jet rolled directly from the runway at Lod Airport into a VIP hangar at the far end of the field. Seconds later a Citroën sedan with smoked windows rolled out of the hangar and through opened gates manned by two Uzi-carrying soldiers.

It was a twenty-minute drive to Tel Aviv. Once through the city, the car turned south on the coast road to Bat Yam. Ten minutes later, it pulled into a basement garage under a two-story villa overlooking the sea.

The villa was owned by a steel company in Pittsburgh, Pennsylvania, which was in turn owned by a holding company in London. The holding company was controlled by the Jarces Bank in Paris.

Nowhere in the ownership papers of the villa was the name of its real owner mentioned: Reba Wallace.

Now she stepped from the Citroën and walked up a short flight of stairs and into a sprawling living room without one person other than two pilots and a driver even seeing her enter the country.

Three men stood and greeted her as she walked into the room and went directly to a paper-strewn table.

There was Aaron Levi, AXE-Mossad liaison, General Zev Cohen, second in command of Mossad, and

Captain Matti Bazri, second in command of Mossad secret special forces unit.

Reba Wallace wasted no time. She opened her briefcase as she returned their greetings and took out a set of notes.

"There is little doubt that Carter and the girl were taken somewhere between the Villa Beirut and the port. Dr. Saisse monitored them via Carter's beeper as far as the Mt. Herman area in the south of Lebanon."

She turned to Captain Bazri. He leaned over a map on the table and used his finger as a pointer. "My two operatives radioed from here, the mouth of the Sa'sa Pass. That was the last we heard of them."

"And there was nothing further from the beeper?" General Cohen asked.

"Nothing," Bazri replied.

Levi sucked air through his teeth and clamped them harder over a small cigar. "So we've got to assume that Carter is with them and up to his ass in trouble."

"Probably," Reba offered, "a safe assumption. From my communiqués with Dr. Saisse, I get the impression that Carter thought he had turned Leila Samir."

"From my experience," Bazri declared, "I'd guess he made a mistake."

Reba frowned. "I know Nick. If he makes a mistake, it's usually a reasonable one, an unseen complication or—"

"The complication," Bazri cut in, "was Leila Samir. She's as slippery as a snake. I'd stake my life on it."

"Maybe so," the woman said. "But if Nick said he thought he had her turned, then I think there's a kernel of truth there and we should go with it."

General Cohen grunted his agreement and leaned over the map himself. "Let's assume they used motorized transportation, and that they have somehow slipped through Syrian and Jordanian patrols. Captain, given that travel time and what we know of the missiles' range, where would that put them?"

"Somewhere here, between Jericho and Na'ur, just north of the Dead Sea." Captain Matti Bazri paused to let this sink in before rolling his eyes up to meet his superior's. "If you're thinking what I think you're think-ing, General, it would have to be a very small team. Jordan isn't Lebanon. If we're caught over the line by a Mukhabarat security team, missiles or no missiles, there will be hell to pay."

"I'm well aware of that," Cohen replied.

"And," Bazri added, "it's like a no-man's-land right there. We have no one on our side in the area, and it's infested with Palestinian supporters."

"Let's say we do go in," Cohen said. "How would you do it?"

"Three people, two disguised as husband and wife. The third their driver. All three fluent in Arabic. We go with papers out of Gibeah in a false-bottom van. We get stopped by Mukhabarat, we're visiting relatives on the Jordan side in Madaba."

"And if you're stopped by Palestinian sympa-thizers?"

"That's where the false bottom in the van enters the picture. Madaba to Gibeah is a regular smuggling route for guns and explosives into Israel. We are on a buying expedition."

General Cohen was silent for several minutes before he turned to the AXE representative. "He's your man, Levi. What do you think?"

Levi pursed his lips in thought for only a moment. "I think if there's any way to stop them, Carter can find it. But even Superman had help now and then."

"It's settled then. How soon can you leave, Captain?"

"Two hours, sir."

"Good," Cohen said. "Make sure your driver is a man who can take those warheads apart."

"I'll do that, sir."

"Two hours," Reba said. "I'll just have time to change."

"Now wait a minute . . ." Bazri said, glaring.

"No, *you* wait a minute, Matti," she retorted. "I speak better Arabic than you do. I'm good in the desert. You should know, you trained me. And if it weren't for my net, you wouldn't know about those missiles in the first place. General?"

Cohen hid a smile. "I'm afraid she's right, Matti. And, besides, if her record could be made public, remember she outranks you. She is a major."

The air was already cooling with the disappearing sun. All of them had moved outside away from the stifling heat of the cottage. All of them except Carter. He remained inside, trussed up like a UPS package.

Twice he heard, even felt, a door open beneath him, and guessed it was an entrance to the missile chamber.

All through the morning and afternoon he had studied the floor and the walls around him. Once more they had let him outside briefly to relieve himself. This time he had protested enough so he was allowed to move into a set of trees by himself. He had taken the time to study the exterior wall further, and the line he could discern of the tracks beneath the sand.

It was a well-constructed if makeshift missile site, and practically undetectable. From any distance it couldn't be spotted at all.

The whole unit obviously rolled out on the tracks.

The dirt floor of the house would be the roof of the dolly, undetectable from the air. It was probably set up on some hydraulic lift that would go up with the missiles. Right up until firing, they would be invisible.

The sun was gone when one of the uglier men came to fetch him. "Rabani wants to see you."

He untied Carter and marched him, his wrists taped, across the sand to a small clump of trees. A tent had been pitched beneath the trees. A blanket had been spread on the ground and food set out.

"Carter, sit and eat," Saif commanded. "We must talk." He spoke as if he were conducting a board meeting.

Carter sat cross-legged between the two women, with Saif directly across from him. The ugly one stood directly behind Carter.

The food was a mutton and rice soup with hard-crusted brown bread. The flavor was nil, but Carter found himself eating it with relish.

As he ate, Saif talked.

"In this sealed envelope are the demands we make on the Israeli government. They are clear and concise, but they are not out of the question."

Carter paused, the spoon halfway to his mouth. "Is one of the demands a joint Israeli-Palestinian government?"

"Yes. Do you think that is an unreasonable demand?"

"Saif, what I think doesn't matter. What they think and do *over there* does. They will never agree to an Israelistine."

Yushi Nuhr leaned forward until she was practically kissing him on the ear. "Then we will send all the Jews *over there* to hell."

Carter went on eating.

Rabani Saif continued. "Three hours before dawn,

Yushi and one of the others will drive you within a mile or so of the Jordan. It will not be a direct route and you will be blindfolded. Even then, if, by some chance, you are able to pinpoint this place to the Israelis, it will do you no good. From the moment you cross the border, the missiles will be armed. If an Israeli assault force comes within two miles of here, I will fire the missiles."

Yushi spoke up. "There is a forty-eight-hour deadline from the time you cross the Jordan."

Saif dropped the envelope on the blanket in front of Carter. "The instructions are also in there on who they must contact, and how, so I will know our demands are being met."

Carter set down his bowl. He moved his eyes from the envelope to rake the three faces around him.

"Forty-eight hours? How stupid are you? How can you possibly expect something of this magnitude to even be discussed, let alone implemented . . ."

In the course of his anger, Carter had gotten to his feet. At a nod from Saif, Yushi had moved away and the guard had moved up beside Carter.

At the height of the speech, the guard turned and drove a fist into the Killmaster's middle. Carter bent forward and almost lost his balance. Then the side of a hand chopped across his neck.

He grunted and hit the ground on his side. Immediately, rough and powerful hands yanked him back to his feet.

"You are in no position to lecture me, Carter," Saif said with a tight grin. "You will do as you are told. Do you understand?"

Carter fought back his mounting anger as he swept them with his watery eyes. Yushi Nuhr's face was impassive. Leila Samir wouldn't look at him.

"Right," Carter gasped.

"I hope so," Saif replied, and nodded again.

The guard went into action again. He clasped his hands together and swung them into Carter's right kidney, in the low back. Carter grunted again in pain and fell to his knees. Then he felt a crushing chop to his neck. Neon signs flashed in the back of his head and he felt himself hit the ground again. He lay there fighting a welling blackness, then the hands were dragging him away.

Behind him, he heard Leila's voice cursing Saif.

Well, he thought, *at least part of her is still on my side.*

Back in the foul-smelling room, the beefy guard threw him in the corner and retied his wrists and ankles. When he was finished, he leaned his face close to Carter.

"You are a lucky man."

"What's your name, besides ugly?" Carter wheezed.

"My name? My name is Mohab."

"Tell you what, Mohab, you're not so lucky."

"Oh? Why is?"

"Because, pretty soon now, I'm going to cut you open from your cock to your belly button."

Then Carter spit in his face.

FIFTEEN

It was after midnight when Carter heard Leila's voice talking to the guard outside the door. Their voices were low. He couldn't make out the words, even if he could have understood them all. But he could determine that they were arguing.

Evidently Leila won, because a few seconds later she entered the room and moved to him. She carried a first aid kit and a glass of steaming mint tea.

"I've come to make sure nothing is broken," she said. "We are not barbarians."

She spoke in a voice louder than necessary, as if it were for the guard's benefit. She also spoke in English.

"Whoopee," Carter said.

"What?"

"Nothing."

"I'm going to untie your hands. Please don't do anything foolish."

She set the kit and the tea on the floor. Then, from her boot she withdrew Carter's stiletto. She held it up for a second, as if she were willing him to inspect it, and then set it down beside the tea. Behind him, her fingers went to work on the knots.

"Take your shirt off," she said, opening the kit and removing rolls of tape and thick wads of gauze.

Carter rubbed his wrists and let them hover just above the stiletto. "I could kill you."

"I know," she said, running her fingers over his back and ribs. "Drink your tea."

It was her game. Carter let her play it her way.

He drank his tea and winced as she applied disinfectant to the cuts the rings on Ugly's fingers had made.

"You may have a cracked rib," she said, unrolling a small blanket of gauze.

"I don't think . . ."

"Shhh, sit up straight." She wrapped the gauze around his chest and extended it clear down to the small of his back. "Hold that in place."

Carter held his arms tightly to his side. Leila readied the tape. With one end of it secure at his side, she picked up the stiletto. He could feel its smooth hilt and part of the blade against his back.

She had slid its hilt up under the gauze.

"Are you going to tell me?" he asked, as she wound the tape tightly around and around his body, keeping the blade in place.

"I will leave about two inches exposed beneath the bandage. When the time comes, that should be enough to cut the line that binds your wrists."

"Leila, I've already figured that out. But why?"

Her teeth caught her lower lip so tightly it seemed that she would draw blood. She poured all of her concentration into the taping, and spoke only when she was nearly finished.

"Rabani and Yushi went off into the sand alone. I knew that they were going to make love. They have done it before, but I had to talk to Rabani. There were too many unanswered questions."

"So you followed them?" Carter murmured.

"Yes. Put your shirt back on. I felt I needed to talk to

him and Yushi alone, so the others couldn't hear."

Carter buttoned his shirt and poked it back into his pants. With his hands he tested the point of the stiletto. It would go through the shirt easily and reach the rope on his wrists.

"Will it work?" she asked.

"Yes. Go on."

"I overheard them talking. Yushi has instructions to kill you."

Carter quickly digested this and all its ramifications. "That means Saif's demands will never reach the Israelis. It probably means he never had any intention of pushing the demands in the first place."

Leila kept her eyes averted, her head down, as she repacked the first aid kit. "He did, in the beginning."

Carter grabbed her by the shoulders and turned her to face him. "But this is now, Leila, *now*. If he doesn't send his demands to the Israelis, what does that tell you?"

Her dark eyes rolled open until they were wide, staring into his. "It means that you were right. The Israelis will never negotiate, and Rabani Saif knows it."

"Exactly," Carter said. "And what else does that tell you?"

When she refused to answer, he shook her in frustration.

"It means, Leila, that he's going to fire those missiles. He's going to start a Middle Eastern holocaust no matter what anyone else does or says."

"I have hidden your Luger in the toolbox in the bed of the truck. Between it and the stiletto, you should be able to protect yourself."

She tried to shake his hands off but he held her steady.

"Leila, if they are going to kill me, why don't they

just do it here? Why go through all this pretense?"

Silence. A film misted over her eyes.

"I think we both know, don't we?" he whispered. "Saif wants you to believe that he is sticking to the original plan. That's it, isn't it?"

Reluctantly she nodded. "There are three parts to the firing sequence. In the original plan, Hashan Akbar set it up so that one part of the sequence would be given to Saif, one to Aman Yassar, and the final one to himself."

Carter released her and slumped against the wall. "And you were the one doing the giving. It was you who set up the three-part sequence in the first place. You are the only one who knows all three."

Again she nodded. "With Akbar and Yassar dead, a contingency clause in the plan went into effect . . ."

Carter finished it for her. He had figured it out. "Saif and Yushi now have two of the sequences, and you have the third. Saif doesn't want you to know that he's planning mass murder, so he sends me to Israel. Only I never get there."

"Put your hands behind your back so I can tie your wrists."

"Leila, he'll torture it out of you. Run, now!"

"I will call the guard."

Carter had no choice at the moment. She tied his hands securely, and stood.

"You were not entirely right about Saif. I think it is Yushi who is mad. Without her influence, I may be able to convince Saif of his folly."

"I wouldn't count on it," Carter growled.

"It is all I have left."

To his surprise, she leaned over and lightly kissed his cheek.

Then she was gone.

•   •   •

The Killmaster lay on his back in the end of the small truck. Through the small rear window of the cab he could see both their heads. Ugly Mohab drove. Yushi Nuhr sat in the passenger seat.

They hadn't bothered to blindfold him after all. But then why should they? He wasn't coming back anyway, any more than he was going to Israel.

During the first half hour of the ride, the woman had glanced back to check on him several times. After she seemed assured that Carter had no intention of throwing himself off the rear of the truck, she kept her eyes forward.

It was a rough ride over sand, rocks, and, now and then, a little-used track. Carter welcomed it. The bouncing around allowed him to get his back closer to the side of the truck bed. Once there, he could steady himself and get some leverage.

Once Hugo's sharp point had pierced his shirt, Carter scrunched his arms up to the small of his back. On the first two tries he missed and sliced the heels of his hands.

The third time he made it and began to saw on the ropes. The stiletto was razor-sharp, so it wasn't long before he felt his wrists part.

Gingerly, he grasped the blade between thumb and forefinger. Despite the chill of the desert night, his back was sweat-slick. The knife slid easily from under the gauze.

He went to work on the rope that bound his ankles. It was tricky. He didn't want to cut all the way through the rope, just enough strands so that when he came off the truck bed he could pop them by yanking his legs apart.

During all of this he had kept track of their position by the stars. The route Mohab had taken was almost due west. Once he had cut north for about three miles, only to head directly west again.

Why not? Carter thought. They didn't fear him pinpointing the missile sight. He wasn't coming back.

When there was only one strand holding his ankles together, he brought the stiletto back up to the small of his back.

He turned his eyes back toward the front. The headlights lit a bumpy, rutted road that seemed to lead toward a black abyss. The longer they drove, the more bumpy, the more primitive it became.

Carter winced as the truck scraped over heavy rocks that kicked up and thumped and banged along the undercarriage. Mohab was heading into hilly country where it appeared no vehicle had ever been before.

As the truck creaked and groaned over one violent bump after another, it threw Carter high enough off the truck bed so he could see Mohab dodging boulders along the dusty trail.

The truck headed down a steep hill toward a black hole of a valley. The thumping from the rocks stopped, to be replaced with a staccato *flap-flap-flap* as they drove into a sand wadi off the rocky trail.

Mohab pulled on the emergency brake and killed the engine. They both got out of the cab and moved around the truck. Carter heard the woman cock the AK-47 she carried.

At the rear of the truck, Yushi Nuhr stood off a couple of feet, the assault rifle across her chest. Mohab moved toward Carter.

"Are we near the river?" Carter asked, holding his ankles tightly together.

"As close as you're going to get," the woman barked. "Put him on the ground!"

The big Arab leaned his rifle against the side of the

truck, put the cigarette he was smoking in his lips, and reached for Carter.

He grabbed the Killmaster by the ankles and yanked him off the truck bed like a side of beef.

Carter howled as his backside scraped painfully over the rough boards. He fell heavily to the sand.

Mohab backed off, leisurely smoking his cigarette. The woman moved in. Carter got to his knees.

"You're going to kill me, aren't you," he said.

The woman smiled. The evil in her face was almost beautiful in its simplicity. "Like a dog."

She was bringing the gun around, when Carter sprang. The stiletto came up like an uppercut. It entered her body just beneath her left breast. Carter felt her blood gush over his hand and forearm.

Her eyes widened and she gasped as the pain followed the shock. By instinct, she slammed the rifle down across Carter's arm.

He hadn't expected it. At the same time, she rolled away from him, pulling the blood-slick hilt of the stiletto from his grasp.

Mohab's reflexes were lightning fast. A howl erupted from his throat as he left his feet in a dive for his own rifle leaning against the truck.

Carter swung in a complete circle. The toe of his boot caught the big man in the middle of his face. Mohab howled in pain and rolled when he hit the sand.

Carter contemplated going for the rifle himself, but Mohab was already back on his feet, charging. The Killmaster set himself to sidestep the bull-like charge and put a knee into the other man's groin.

He didn't expect what happened.

Mohab paused in mid-charge and moved into a fighter's stance, a wolfish grin twisting his ugly lips.

"This is better. I will beat you to death with my hands."

Carter was surprised, too surprised. Before he knew it, his head was rocked back with a couple of stinging punches that landed over his right eye.

Blood immediately filled his eyes. He shook his head to clear it.

He couldn't believe the incongruity of it as Mohab moved around him, cutting him off from both rifles. The man actually meant what he said: he was going to kill Carter with his bare hands.

All Carter could do was fight fire with fire and try to maneuver himself back toward one of the rifles. This would be easier said than done. Mohab had fifty pounds and five inches of reach on him. And the man glided in the soft sand like a snake.

Carter threw himself forward. Mohab went low, bobbed to his left, and let Carter's clubbing right hand go past. The Arab leaned into his own right and dug it into Carter's body just under the ribs. Carter turned and the hook caught him with the weight of Mohab's big body behind it.

Carter shook his head. Blood seeped down from a split eyebrow. The left hand rapped him twice, three more times before he could pull his head behind a shoulder.

The Arab was good.

"Come!" the big man taunted, a leering grin curving his thick lips. "Do not back up! Fight!"

Pivoting, Carter aimed a kick at his kneecap, a savage sweep of the foot that would have crippled him if it had landed. Mohab stuck the left into Carter's mouth, shifted it to the sore right eye, and hooked off the jab as he skipped away. Carter plodded after, pulling air into his lungs, knowing already the first heaviness in his legs, needing to close with Mohab to hold him and work him over before he could pull away. Mohab had to be slowed down.

The left again, educated, a slashing weapon that was cutting Carter's face to pieces.

Carter lunged, tried to go into a shell as he came in, but Mohab stabbed and coasted back, stabbed and stopped momentarily to bang both hands to Carter's body, to switch the jolting hook to Carter's jaw. Then he was gone again.

Carter focused on the man's smirking face, on the untouched face with the coldly mocking eyes. Head down, he rammed in and almost caught Mohab solidly. His head glanced off the Arab's ribs, but when he tried to wrap an arm around his belly, something exploded against the back of his neck.

He fell, and a heavy boot ground his face into the sand. He sensed the other foot going back. Mohab was going to kick his skull in.

Carter hooked a desperate hand around an ankle and snapped it down and away. Mohab fought for balance, hissing like a cornered rattlesnake. He went down, but not hard, still good with his weight, still quick. He was rolling over when Carter got him in the back with a knee.

The big man yelped in shock, clawed at the truck to pull himself out from under the sudden pain. Carter hit him twice, then again, both hands chopping behind the head, both hands driving Mohab into the sand.

But the man was tough. He was hard and rugged, and proved it by arching violently to hands and knees, by throwing Carter off his back. He scuttled away as Carter tried to grab him again, and used the truck to climb up. When he turned, Carter saw where the rough metal had scraped his face raw on one side, saw the new angle of Mohab's nose, the leaking blood.

He came off the back of the truck, using it as a fulcrum. He butted Carter in the face, but the Killmaster was past feeling blows. He rocked with it and chopped Mohab along the neck, then got his knee into the man's crotch. Mohab stopped. He lowered his head to Carter's pumping chest and hung on, wrapping his thick arms around Carter so he could stay on his feet.

Gulping a lungful of air, Carter pulled his arms free and got the right one around the Arab's neck in a headlock, anchoring the grip with his other hand. Mohab was tough. He'd taken the pain and the hammering and hadn't begged for mercy; he hadn't cried uncle.

But Carter saw that it wouldn't take much now to finish him.

He took a faltering run at the truck, with Mohab's head sticking out of his grip. Carter wobbled at the smash, used his hip to keep Mohab up, and backed away for another swaying try at the truck bed.

The second smash accomplished its purpose. Under Carter's left arm Mohab's head cracked sickeningly against the rear of the truck. When the Killmaster let him drop limply to the sand, Mohab's eyes were rolling and the top of his skull was spongy.

Carter leaned against the truck, gasping for air. His left eye was blinded by blood now, and there was a mist in front of the right one. There wasn't a bone or muscle in his body that didn't scream with pain, and his legs felt as though they were hollow and filled with water.

He had to concentrate to keep from blacking out. It was unbelievable, but Mohab was still moving. Laboriously, the man crawled to one knee. Then he defied gravity and got to his feet.

Impossible, Carter thought, *the man is dead!*

To make it all worse, he heard a sound to his left. He turned and saw Yushi Nuhr. Somehow she was still alive, the stiletto protruding from beneath her breast.

She had crawled to her rifle and was trying to bring it into a position to fire.

"Give it up!" Carter gasped. "You're dead, or you should be!"

She was superhuman. It was as if she were a zombie, the walking dead. Her face was bloodless, the eyes already milky white. Yet she managed to lift the rifle.

At the same time, Mohab aped her. Like a robot he headed for Carter, his big paws in front of him, the fingers curling in anticipation of the Killmaster's throat.

It took Carter's last ounce of strength. He stumbled to the woman and grabbed the gun.

Useless.

Her grip on the rifle was with all the strength of death. The muzzle continued to roll in his direction. Behind him, he could hear Mohab's plodding steps toward him in the sand.

"Jesus," Carter croaked.

He lunged at the woman. He took her by her slender bird's throat with one hand, his thumb pushed in behind the point of her jawbone to paralyze her, his fingers cutting her wind. She could only pull without strength at his wrist, trying to take some of the pressure off the nerve center. It was instinctive but ineffectual. Only a counterattack against another nerve center, the testicles most vulnerable of all, could have broken his hold, and he held her in a way to defend himself against that. When she was helpless, he spun her into the deadly curve of his arms.

Laboriously, he lifted his knee into her back and bent her until he heard the neck snap.

Just before he pushed the woman's lifeless body into

Mohab, he withdrew the stiletto from her breast.

The big Arab had to be sightless, but he shoved her off by instinct and kept staggering toward Carter. He grunted as he moved, saliva and blood drooling from the corners of his mouth.

But still he came.

Carter staggered himself. He moved his feet wide apart, the right foot a few inches behind the left for balance.

When Mohab embraced him, Carter buried the stiletto in his groin. With his last effort, he yanked upward, twisting the blade at the same time, disemboweling the big Arab.

There was no scream of agony, no wrenching of the body.

The man was already dead. He slid down Carter's front, leaving a bloody trail in his wake.

The Killmaster took two faltering steps and fell across both their bodies.

SIXTEEN

Carter didn't know where he was. He seemed to be floating. But he could feel the two bodies beneath him. He could also smell the rancid odor of sun-baked blood.

At first he thought he was dead. Then he surmised that the two bodies beneath him were just that, bodies. They were dead, and he knew it, so he must be alive.

He could hear the wings of the vultures as they settled around him. Beyond them he saw the hyenas arriving, and the jackals.

Friendly, he thought, the cleanup crew was friendly.

The vultures moved in. One of the dogs turned and chased a hyena, snapping at his rump.

Take your turn, fellas.

Then he was looking directly into the beady yellow and black eye of a vulture. There was a grin on the bastard's beak as he leaned forward to pick the first piece of flesh.

Carter screamed and came awake.

"Nick, Nick, it's all right. You're safe . . . you're all right!"

It was a she. And she was between his eyes and sunlight streaming through a window. The streaks of harsh light painted her breasts and hips a molten mixture of olive skin and dark eyes and sulky mouth.

"Mmm, nice," he murmured. "Very nice."

"Nick . . . it's me."

He forced one eye to focus. "Reba?"

"Yes."

"Are you in my dream?"

"No, darling, I'm real."

"Water."

He gagged on the first mouthful, got the whole glass down on the second try, and asked for another.

"Where are we?"

"A sheep herder's hut near Mount Nebo."

"Oh? What the hell are you doing here?"

"We were doing a north-south zigzag, ten miles on each leg. We saw the vultures circling, and investigated."

"Oh. Then there were vultures."

"Nick . . ."

"Huh?"

"How many fingers?"

"Three. Your breasts are beautiful. Why are you naked?"

"Because it's almost a hundred and twenty degrees outside. We buried the other two and laid up here until you came out of it."

"Yushi Nuhr and Mohab."

"What?"

"That's who you buried."

"Oh. It was pretty hard to recognize them. Luckily, evidently you kept moving. They tore the others apart without even touching you."

"Jesus."

There was a knock on the door. "Reba?"

"Yes."

"Is he awake?"

"Yes, just a minute."

She walked the length of the room to pick up a white robe. As his eyes watched her move, he knew beyond any doubt that he was alive. Her stomach was flat, the waist firm, her thighs slim with the outline of a brief bikini imprinted in white on her buttocks.

"God, you're beautiful," he croaked.

"Don't tell me I'm turning you on now?"

"Always," he chuckled.

She opened the door and two dark, well-built men dressed in only their shorts moved to the side of the bed.

"How do you feel, Carter?"

"Like hell. Who the hell are you?"

"Captain Matti Bazri, Mossad special forces. This is Eli Meir."

"What are you doing in Jordan?"

"Looking for you," Bazri said with a broad smile. He pulled a chair to the side of the bed and straddled it, facing Carter. "Want to tell us about it?"

Other than the cut over Carter's eye, the bruises were no worse than many he had endured in the past. By midafternoon, he was up and walking around. By dusk he was ready to go.

There was no zigzagging on the return trip. Carter, with Reba in the passenger seat beside him, drove the old truck. Captain Bazri and Eli Meir followed in the van. He navigated by the stars, and pulled up about four miles short of the site.

In the compartment under the van's floorboard, Bazri had brought enough to equip a small army.

Carter vetoed the grenades, their launchers, and the small mortars.

"Anything this big going in there randomly, and God knows what we might blow up. Right?"

The weapons expert, Eli Meir, agreed. "If those missiles are jerry-rigged without an absolute professional arming them, it's impossible to tell what will set them off."

They decided on the AK-47s Bazri had brought from the storehouse of captured arms kept in the armory outside Haifa. Each of them wore a utility belt with a commando knife, a side arm, and four extra clips for the Kalashnikovs.

Armed, they moved to the bed of the truck. Meir spread out a section map of the area, and Bazri wielded a small penlight while Carter gave them a rundown.

"The site is a large shepherd's cottage about here. I don't think I'm more than a hundred yards off. Captain, if you'll take Meir and skirt the area, staying three to four miles out, they won't detect you."

Bazri nodded. "Drop Meir off about here?"

"Good," Carter said. "You head on and come in on foot from here. Reba and I will come in from this position, due west. We'll have them in a pincer on three sides . . . east, west, and south. There's a deep wadi to the north. If they do run, they'll have to go that way . . . and it's a dead end."

"What about vehicles?" Reba asked.

"They had only the truck," Carter replied. "Others could have come in since I left, but I don't think so. Saif is running his own private little war now. The less people involved, the more secrecy for him."

"So their strength now is five?"

Carter grimly folded the map and handed it to Bazri. "Not really. I think Leila Samir's game when I left was to hold out on Saif. If she's held out this long, I imagine he's given up all pretenses of adhering to the original plan."

"What does that mean?" Reba asked.

"It means that Saif is probably torturing her into giving him her third of the fusing sequence. That's why I'll go in first. Don't start raising hell until I do. Agreed?"

All three of them nodded.

Bazri and Meir headed for the van.

Carter waited until the sound of the engine had faded in the distance before he turned to Reba.

"Stay a hundred yards behind me all the way. Never lose sight. They'll have a sentry out somewhere. Get him when he spots me, and do it quietly."

She nodded and slung the rifle. Carter chuckled.

"What's the matter with you?"

"Nothing," he said. "I just remember you a few nights ago in that red dress. If uppercrust London could see you now."

She grinned. "Move, Carter, before I change my mind."

He took off across the sand. She waited until he was a recognizable blur in the moonlight, and followed.

It happened just after Carter was taken away. Saif and the other three men moved in a circle around her as she crouched by the fire, eating.

"It's time now, Leila."

She looked up innocently. "Time for what, Rabani?"

"The proper connections for the wires," he replied. "The final sequence of numbers that will fuse the missiles."

"There is no need of that until Carter has reached the Israelis."

Saif dropped into a crouch beside her. The other three men tightened up the circle.

"No, Leila. I want to arm the missiles now."

Calmly, she set the tin plate on the ground and blankly returned his stare. "No, Rabani."

"Leila, I am in command now."

She had the Beretta in a holster on her belt. An AK-47 was by her knee. She rolled away, grabbing for the rifle with one hand and pulling the Beretta with the other.

The Beretta was kicked from her hand and a pair of boots landed on the barrel of the rifle, holding and driving it into the sand.

She managed to avoid their clawing hands, and got to her feet. They ringed her. Leila backed away from them, crouching and glaring from one to the other. The odds against her were overwhelming.

"Don't be a fool, Saif," she hissed.

"It is you, Leila, who plays the fool. My way is the only way . . . now."

He lifted his hand. In it was a coil of rope. He spoke grimly: "It shall be the way you want it, Leila. We can be reasonable. But if you want pain, we will provide it."

"Don't you see what he's doing?" Leila cried to the others. "He would end the world for all of us!"

Their faces were immobile, impassive. They said nothing. Only then did Leila realize what fanatics they had all become.

Saif nodded to them and they all moved in on her slowly, spreading out so she couldn't watch them all at the same time. Suddenly one ran in at her. Leila turned swiftly and lashed out. The heel of her hand pounded flesh, but the next split second the rest of them hit her solidly and simultaneously. Sheer weight of numbers bore her to the ground. But she fought with insane desperation as fists and boots thudded down on her.

"You bastards!" she screamed.

Her hands were protecting her head but a fist pounded into her unprotected stomach. The breath left her body, leaving her gasping painfully on the ground.

"You will tell us, Leila," Saif hissed. "In time you will tell us."

She tried to resist, but it was hopeless. They tied lengths of cord around each wrist and forced her to an outside wall of the cottage. Two iron rings once used to tie up livestock were cemented into the wall high up and far apart.

"Rabani," she gasped, "don't do this!"

The men paused, looking to their leader. His face was a stoic mask as he moved it closer to hers.

"The Israelis will never negotiate, Leila. Carter was right. We have no other way. Well?"

She glared into his glittering eyes. "He was right about something else," she whispered. "You are mad."

He returned her stare for a long moment, then gestured to the men. "Do it," he growled.

They passed the ends of the cords through the iron rings and heaved on them, drawing Leila upward until the very tips of her toes barely touched the ground.

She cried out in pain as they tied off the ends of the cords. It felt as though she were being split apart. Her arms were being torn from their sockets. Her chest was constricted until she couldn't breathe and the cords bit into her wrists until blood ran down her arms.

The four of them moved away. They squatted by the fire and smoked silently for twenty minutes.

Then one of them stood and moved to a bucket of water. From the bucket he took a heavy length of hemp that had been soaking. He twisted it until the water was wrung from it, and returned to the fire.

A few minutes later, Saif took the length of hemp and returned to her. "The numbers, Leila, the numbers."

"No! You'll have to kill me, Rabani!"

"How many times have you seen this done, woman?"

he sneered. "You know you won't die. You will only suffer ten hells."

Sweat ran down her face and dripped from the tip of her chin. The pain was already unbearable, but she refused to cry out. She let her head fall forward until it rested against the cool stone of the wall.

Saif locked his fingers in her hair and jerked her head around to show her the hemp whip.

"I'll start with the back, Leila. And if you remain silent, I'll turn you around."

She closed her eyes and whispered down curses upon him, his family, and all the sons he would never breed because he didn't have the balls of a man.

"I'll cut you in two, you bitch."

A knife opened the khaki shirt she wore, splitting it in half. It fell apart and she felt the cool night air on her bare flesh.

"You'll talk," he hissed.

"I have already forgotten everything you want to know."

"You'll remember."

They all moved back then, leaving a semicircle around her.

Saif took off his djellaba and tossed it to one of the men. The muscles of his powerful arms rippled smoothly as he rolled up his shirt sleeves. He picked up the whip, stood behind her, and rested the pliant lash across her shoulders so that he could gauge his distance.

"You want to talk now?"

The mere touch of the lash turned her blood cold. She needed all her self-control to restrain herself from jibbering.

She remained silent.

The weight of her hanging body pressed her chest

against the cold stone wall, and there was a sob of utter helplessness inside her.

There was a tense and electrified silence.

Leila heard the creak of boots and Saif's deep intake of breath as he swung his arm back high. Then he grunted with the effort he exerted. The whip swished and whistled in the air and then the lash bit into flesh with a meaty *thwack*.

Leila heard it land before she felt it. That was the strange thing. But there was only a split second between the two sensations and then the burning, screaming agony sent her out of her mind. She writhed and shrieked and thrashed around without knowing she was doing it.

The tip of the whip curled over her shoulder. It left a weal a quarter of an inch wide. The lash cut diagonally downward across her shoulder and spine to the region of her left kidney where the weal was an inch wide. For the entire length of the weal, flesh was scooped out, leaving a furrow from which blood gushed freely.

She tried to count the strokes before she passed out. But they all become one . . . one long lash of agony.

SEVENTEEN

The moon was like a majestic Venetian gondola standing on its end. The sky was clear and the stars were bright. Now and then a gust of wind swirled the sand around him into a whooshing mini-funnel.

Other than that, there was no sound.

There had been rise after rise of sand, rocks, and scrub trees. Each seemed to be the last, only to be topped to disclose yet another behind it, and yet another after that.

The sweat was dripping down his face and his limbs were talking back to him from slogging through the sand.

Then, suddenly, quite close, no more than a couple of hundred yards away, there it was, the rear of the cottage. The area to the left, north, was dark. No matter how Carter strained his eyes he could see no movement and his ears heard no sound.

He looked back to find Reba. It wasn't easy. Bazri had trained her well. Finally he spotted her, crouching in the natural cover of a boulder, peering through the rocks at the cottage. She used her cover as naturally as an animal.

Carter used his hands to tell her that the original plan was out. Evidently, Saif was so sure of his position that he had posted no guards on the outlying perimeters of the cottage.

Without a sound, she covered the ground between them and dropped to her side by Carter.

He pointed to the glow of a fire to the right of the cottage.

"There's a tent in a grove of trees around there," he whispered, his lips at her ear. "That's where the glow of the fire is coming from."

"Are they all there?" she whispered back.

"Have to find out."

She touched his shoulder and pointed. "Is that the wall that moves out?"

He nodded. "There are tracks under the sand."

Their eyes met, conveying the same thought. If the missiles were still under cover, Leila Samir had managed to hold out.

Suddenly a bone-chilling scream pierced the night. It was loud in the empty silence, loud enough, it seemed, to reach for miles.

Instinctively, Carter winced away from the sharp sting of it. He could guess its source.

He squeezed Reba's shoulder and signed for her to hold her position.

She shook her head.

Yes, he nodded emphatically as he got quickly to his feet and ran across an open space to a clump of rocks that lay a little to the south. He looked back at Reba and saw her nod of approval.

Again he signaled her to stay where she was, but she shook her head and came running over, moving fast, lithely and silently, like an animal. She slithered to a crouch as she reached him.

"Oh, my God," she gasped in a strangled whisper.

Two men sat on their haunches by the fire. Smoke curled upward from cigarettes between their lips.

Rabani Saif stood by the wall. He was naked to the

waist and sweat gleamed like oil on his chest and shoulders. A length of thick rope hung from the hand at his side.

Hanging from thick hooks embedded in the wall was Leila Samir. She, too, was naked to the waist, the remnants of a khaki shirt shredded at her feet. Her back and arms were bloody pulp.

Carter boiled.

"Nick," Reba whispered, "easy. She's as good as dead."

The words were scarcely out of her mouth when Saif barked a command to the men squatting by the fire.

"Water! The bitch has passed out again."

One of the two men lurched to his feet. At the wall, he grabbed a bucket of water and ran to Leila. He upended the bucket over her head.

Instantly the night was filled with another of her screams. Saif moved in close to her. He spoke in low tones directly into her ear, too low for Carter and Reba to hear what was said.

"She's still alive," Carter murmured, more to himself than to the woman beside him.

He consulted his watch. It would be another fifteen, perhaps twenty minutes before Bazri and Meir would be in position.

Too long.

By then Leila Samir would be dead. Or, worse yet, she would give up and tell Saif the information he needed.

Again Carter checked the situation. Saif with his whip, no arms. One man refilling the bucket at the well. He carried a side arm in a holster at his belt. The third man still crouched by the fire. He cradled an AK-47 across his knees.

Where was the fourth man?

No matter, Carter thought; it was now or never. They couldn't wait for Bazri and Meir.

"Reba . . ." he hissed.

"Yes." She moved her ear to his lips.

"Move over there, among those larger rocks. When I give the signal, you take out the one at the well. I'll get the one at the campfire."

"Then what?"

"I'll rush Saif . . ."

"He'll kill her."

Carter shook his head. "Don't think so. He needs what's in her head too much. Killing her now would ruin his whole plan. Go!"

Reba slithered away like a snake. In seconds she had a shooting place among the larger rocks. She looked back and Carter nodded.

Slowly he moved up over the rock hiding him and stretched the rifle out over the top. He flicked off the safety and . . .

From a high window in the cottage, just above the rings holding Leila, there was a garbled shout in Arabic.

It was the fourth man. Even as Carter rolled to safety, the man's rifle chattered. Four or five bullets pumped at him carelessly, but one of them found the funnel of sheltering stones. It ricocheted round and round savagely in the confined space before it went singing off into the night.

Carter pulled himself deeper into the shadow. He lay there for a moment on his side peering over his shoulder.

The one by the campfire had dived into the trees. He was returning Reba's fire.

She had hit the one at the well, but he was still alive. Bullets from Reba's rifle kicked up sand all around him, but he too was firing back.

From his position, Carter couldn't see Saif and Leila. The fourth man at the window was also in a blind spot. He rolled over onto his stomach and peered around the corner of the rock.

There was a sudden burst of fire again, six shots fired in rapid succession. He was finding the range now, shooting lower. The bullets spattered in the loose sand and sent up hot little clouds of angry dust close beside Carter.

"Reba!" he shouted. "The window!"

She nodded her understanding. The angle of her rifle shifted and she laid down covering fire.

Carter got to his feet quickly and ran around to the north again, feeling a heightened alarm as the shots that came after him were suddenly closer than they had been before, as though desperation was forcing a kind of careful accuracy on the man holed up inside. One of them struck no more than an inch from Carter's foot as he fell to the ground behind a rough rock table.

He looked back and saw Reba raising her head to look at the cottage. Instantly there was more firing from the trees and behind the wall.

Carter frantically signaled her to keep down. She shifted her position, looked across at him, and raised her finger in warning. The finger was going around and around.

Carter was heading for the north wall and the window on that side. Reba was telling him that the shooter in the cottage had guessed his intent and moved himself.

Carter nodded his understanding and took off again. He moved to the north about thirty yards and dropped.

There was no fire.

He inched his way forward, moving carefully from cover to cover, keeping the window under careful observation. He waited for the shooting to start again.

It didn't.

He exposed himself for a brief instant as he slipped from the rocks and dropped to the sand. He was in full view of the window, but there was no fire.

In a final dash he was there, pressed up close against the heavy stones of the cottage. He could feel their roughness through his clothes.

He was close now, close enough to see the rusted nails that held the light planks half across the window opening, to see where they had been carelessly pulled away to let in the light again. Inside, all was quiet.

He had a sudden premonition, wondering if the final shot he had heard . . .

And then there was a whimpering sound, very faint, coming from the other side of the weathered boards that stood between him and his quarry. It was like a woman crying, or rather trying not to cry and merely stifling a sound in her throat.

Carter slung his rifle. He loosened the Luger in its leather sheath and cautiously reached upward for the windowsill. When his fingers curled around it, he soundlessly pulled himself up until he could peer into the room.

The first thing he saw was the man's assault rifle. It was lying on the floor by the south window.

Then he saw the man. He was sitting in the corner, on his heels, crouched down, his angular knees jutting up, and his head bowed deep between them. His hands, long-fingered, thin, blue-veined, were covering his face, and the sound that came from under them was frightening. It was soft, like a muted moan, but drawn-out like a baby's crying, a whimpering noise of desperate agony.

Carter dropped into the room.

The man heard the scraping noise of Carter's boots. His face, or what was left of it, came up out of his hands.

Reba hadn't missed.

One side of his face was gone. The other was a bloody mess, a dark hole where the eye had been.

He went for the side arm at his hip and fired at where he had heard the sound of Carter's boots.

The Killmaster had already moved, drawing the Luger.

Four explosions echoed in the room. The fourth was Carter's. It hit the man in the center of the chest.

It was actually a mercy killing. He wouldn't have lived another five minutes . . . and those five minutes would have seemed an eternity of unspeakable pain.

Carter sheathed the Luger, unslung the rifle, and moved to the window.

The firing below had stopped. Then he saw why. The two men were crawling silently through the moonlight. Reba had moved further into the rocks and they were flanking her.

Carter set the rifle on the sill and zeroed in on the nearest man.

"Reba!" he shouted, and fired.

The man cried out and rolled to his back, his Kalashnikov spewing toward the window and Carter.

Carter fired twice more and the man lay still.

The other one rolled behind some rocks and alternated his fire between Carter and Reba.

Carter chanced a quick look over the side. Ropes hung limply from the two steel rings.

Saif had cut Leila Samir down.

But where were they?

The man didn't have a chance. Reba kept him contained with short bursts while Carter popped at him with the advantage of height and visibility.

It was the big, bearded one who had been crouching

by the fire when they had first opened up. He was pinned down now, and it was only a matter of time.

Carter's shots, as well as Reba's, kept getting closer and closer.

"Give up!" Carter shouted.

His answer was a volley from the rocks, and then a scream in Arabic as the man stood up in full view.

Insane, Carter thought, as he watched the man run directly toward Reba. It was a suicide course. He was running directly toward where she lay securely behind a huge rock.

Carter sighted his rifle on the running figure, but he knew there would be no need to fire.

Reba waited until the last possible instant. Then she calmly stood, orange flame erupting from the end of her rifle.

The man was practically cut in half as he hit the ground.

She turned and motioned to Carter.

"What is it?" Carter shouted.

She motioned again. But before he got the picture, he heard a roar from below him. A great, jagged hole erupted in the dirt floor beneath him.

This wasn't a rifle. It was something bigger, much bigger . . . more like a bazooka.

Suddenly he knew where Rabani Saif was.

Another explosion, and then another, and another, tracing an exploring pattern toward the angle of his cover. Carter thought the man below must be using a bazooka, a weapon with a stopping power far more terrible than his rifle. The shots pierced the ceiling of the floor below, then the joists and floorboards, and still came through with enough force to slam into the walls and ceiling.

There was a pause.

Carter wondered how long it would take the man to

reload. He had no doubt at all that if one of the shells came anywhere near him through the dirt floor, he would be dead.

Without waiting for the next burst, Carter dived from the window. He hit the sand bent-legged, rolled, and came back up on his feet running.

Reba was moving closer, still using the rocks as a shield.

Carter dived and came down on his belly beside her. He gasped air into his lungs as she sprayed the open door into the missile chamber.

"Knock it off," he managed to gasp. "God knows what you're liable to hit in there."

She stopped firing and dropped down beside him, jacking a fresh clip into the AK-47.

"You all right?"

"Yeah," Carter wheezed. "You?"

"Fit as a fiddle, darling. What the hell has he got in there anyway?"

"Don't know. Antitank gun, bazooka . . . hard to tell. But it's a hell of a lot of firepower."

"Jesus," she moaned, "without grenades, it could take hours to get him out of there."

Carter started to roll onto his belly for a look-see, when a moving blur appeared twenty yards to their rear.

He was bringing up his rifle when Bazri stepped from the trees, his arms to his side. Meir appeared close behind him.

"Come on in, hurry!" Carter shouted.

The two men dropped to their bellies and wriggled up to join Carter and Reba.

"Sorry we're late," Bazri groaned.

"You're not late," Carter said. "We just had to start without you."

"What's up?" Meir asked.

Carter explained.

Reba added, "He cut her down the minute the firing started, and carried her inside. I didn't dare fire—I would have hit her."

The three men looked at each other.

That is exactly what she should have done . . . fired, and cut them both down before Saif got to the missiles.

But they said nothing.

Reba averted her eyes.

"What are our options?" Bazri asked.

"Damn few," Carter growled, lighting a cigarette and dragging deeply. "First out, you and Meir get on the north and east sides. We'll have him surrounded. Reba, you on the west. I'll take the south."

Her brows met in a vee. "And then?"

"I'll reach the door," he replied. "You three come in as backup. He can't take us all, no matter how much firepower he's got."

Reba exchanged solemn glances with the two Israelis. "That means he's got more than a fifty-fifty chance of taking out at least the first two through the door."

"That's right," Carter said. "Now get moving."

Carter hit the door firing. He expended a whole clip from the assault rifle on the lock mechanism. The wood around it shattered and the entire door gave way under his shoulder.

He hit the concrete floor of the missile chamber and rolled. When he came up on his knees, he jammed a fresh clip into the AK-47 and chambered a shell.

But when he brought it up, he could see there was nothing to fire at.

There were five of them, antitank guns. They were mounted on stanchions pointing straight up through the roof. A fuse line had been run through the trigger mechanism of each one.

Leila Samir's tortured form lay between the two missiles. She appeared to be still breathing, but just barely.

In front of the missiles, Carter saw the crack of light where the dolly had been moved out. The space was just big enough for a man to crawl through.

"Bazri . . . Meir, come in!"

The two of them tumbled through the door, with Reba right on their heels.

"Saif's gone," Carter hissed. "He rigged these guns as a diversion and slipped out."

"Dammit!" Bazri roared.

"No time to worry about it now," Carter said. "Fan out, two directions, west and south. Chances are he'll try for our transportation, and he'll figure we came from one of those two directions."

They moved, fast. Meir went south. Carter and Bazri went west toward the vehicles. Reba stayed behind to do what she could for Leila Samir and to make sure Saif didn't double back.

It took less than an hour. They picked up his trail at once in the sand, but they knew they were too late.

This was confirmed when they reached the wadi where they had left the vehicles.

The truck was gone.

Eli Meir crawled down from the ladder with a sigh. Carter crushed out his cigarette and got to his feet.

"Well?"

"He couldn't lug the warheads, but he did manage to take the most important components."

"What does that mean?" Carter asked in disgust.

"I think you know."

"Tell me, dammit!"

"It means, given an expert and the raw materials, Saif can build two more of these as soon as he gets himself set up again."

"Shit," Carter cursed. "Just shit, shit, shit!"

He stormed outside.

"Well?" Bazri asked.

Carter told him.

The Israeli dropped to his butt in the sand by the van. "So, the damn thing starts all over again."

Carter's throat was clogged with disgust. He couldn't manage a reply. He moved around to the rear of the van. Leila was stretched out on the floor of the van. Reba was doing the best she could.

"How is she?"

"Not good. She's in and out of shock. He beat the hell out of her. She needs a doctor and a hospital."

Carter nodded. "She would know where Saif would go to get a new start on his wild scheme. Can you keep her alive until we get back into Israel?"

"I'm gonna try."

"Don't try," Carter growled, "*do* it!"

"You're a hard son of a bitch, Carter," she said levelly.

"I know it," he said, and moved back around the van. "Bazri . . ."

"Yeah?"

"Get some plastique. Let's blow this place to hell and get out of here."

EIGHTEEN

The hot sun off the Gulf of Aqaba warmed Carter's back while he lay facedown on the pier in back of the villa. A powerboat strained at her mooring ropes while the stanchions groaned. Waves lapped beneath him. Without moving or opening his eyes, he reached for the beer bottle, overshot, and instead touched Reba's thigh.

"Sorry," he murmured, "went for my beer and missed."

"Open your eyes," she chuckled. The sun made her no less indolent; she lay on her stomach, the top of her swimsuit loosened so the sun wouldn't leave a mark on her smooth back.

"If I open my eyes, I'll see where I am and get more pissed."

"Is it so bad?" she sighed. "Coral Beach, private villa, the glittery playground of Eilat . . . me?"

"Yes," Carter said bitterly.

A week of enforced paradise had strained his sense of proportion. He itched to move on, get it over with for good.

He found his beer and drank, letting his eyes drift across the bay to the Jordanian port city of Aqaba.

Somewhere over there was Rabani Saif.

After blowing up the compound, Carter had driven

the van like a wild man to the Jordan River, then cut
south to the Allenby Bridge. Bazri had found a phone
that worked and made frantic phone calls so they
wouldn't be stopped on the Jordan side of the river.

Once into Israel, a helicopter had been waiting. They
flew directly to Tel Aviv, where a team of doctors had
gone to work on Leila Samir.

Carter and Reba had continued on to Eilat and the
security of the government-owned villa.

Since then, Carter had lain by the pool, lain on the
pier, and brooded.

It was the Mossad's gig now, and all he could do was
wait.

Bazri and General Cohen had promised Carter that
when the time came he would be in on the kill.

That had been four days ago, when they had come to
tell him that their intelligence sources had a tip. Saif had
gone south. He had friends in Aqaba. Leila had surfaced
from her coma long enough to confirm that information.

Now Saif was in a tent city somewhere south of
Aqaba. For all intents and purposes, he was completely
safe. The Jordanians really didn't want him around, but
they wouldn't do anything about him being there.

"I know what's wrong with you," Reba said.

"You do?"

"You need a woman."

Carter opened his eyes. She had rolled to her side,
her arms wide, her bare breasts gleaming invitingly.
They reminded him of Mexican mangoes in season, ri-
pened to a golden glow.

They hadn't made love since arriving at the villa.
Not for lack of trying, but Carter couldn't shove the rest
of it out of his mind.

"When it's over," he said, closing his eyes again.

"Shit," she said, and dropped back to the blanket.

"Mr. Carter?"

He looked up. It was their Mossad bodyguard in houseboy's garb. He was just a little man, dark, a Sephardic Jew from Morocco, but Bazri had said he was deadly.

Carter believed it. He had worked out with the man.

"Yes?"

"They're here."

"Thank God," Reba sighed.

Carter was on his feet immediately, gathering up his cigarettes, his lighter, and his beer. He gave her back, legs, and rear end a last glance, and moved down the pier onto the grass, past the sprinklers and on to the veranda that led into the villa. The sun had bleached his dark body hair white. A few gray streaks glinted in his head of black hair.

Bazri was waiting in the study. Carter flopped into a chair across from him.

"I hope this is business and not pleasure."

"It is," the Israeli said. "We've located him right where Leila said he would be."

"The tent city?"

"Right. Still can't get to him, of course, but our people have a wrinkle."

Carter leaned forward in anticipation. "Let's hear it."

"He's moving into Aqaba for one night."

"When?"

"Tonight," Bazri replied. "The Hotel Sahara, under the name of Fezzaz. It's a suite on the eighth floor. Word has it that men of his persuasion are coming in from all over the Middle East."

Carter cursed. "So he's putting another try together."

"Looks that way. Our research people figure we do have one advantage."

"Yeah?" Carter said. "What is that?"

"Ego," Bazri replied. "He's probably hidden the

components, and only he knows where they are."

"That would fit," the Killmaster said, nodding grimly. "He's got an image of himself as the great martyr."

"Exactly."

"Can we get to him?" Carter asked.

Bazri nodded. "We think so. We've put a plan together. Go in off the gulf tonight using the launch."

"Yes."

"It will have to be a one-shot kill. It can be done from the office building across the street."

Bazri spread out a scale map of the street and the two buildings. In detail, he laid out the plan. Carter nodded with satisfaction.

"Looks good. How do I get out?"

Bazri smiled. "You?"

"Who else?"

"Me."

Carter shook his head. "Not your line. You're a team player. This kind of thing is my daily bread."

The Israeli's grin broadened. "I know. I just wanted to hear you say it. Okay, once it's done, there will be a sheep truck, here, a block from the hotel. The truck will take you south to the no-man's-land between Jordan and Saudi Arabia. We don't think there will be much of a chase. They want to get rid of him as much as we do."

"Where do I go from there?"

"Just after dark, an amphibious helicopter. You swim to it. We'll have him as close in as possible. You in?"

"Up to my ass," Carter said, grinning.

Bazri folded the maps and handed them to Carter. "We leave at midnight. Get some rest."

Carter practically ran up the stairs to his bedroom. He peeled off his swim trunks and took a shower.

When he emerged from the bathroom, a towel draped

around his middle, she was standing at the foot of the bed.

"Well?"

"Well what?" he said.

"Are you well?"

He grinned. "Very."

"Then help me get more comfortable." Her eyes were bright with excitement. She leaned over and crushed out her unfinished cigarette, then straightened, walking toward him, supple hips swaying and a daring, mischievous smile playing on her moist, red lips. "Help me?"

"Help you?"

"The suit, silly. It has a long back zipper and it's a real effort for me to reach around and pull down on it."

She stopped close in front of him, the thrusting tips of her big breasts centered on his chest. Then she deliberately turned her back so that the talon of the swimsuit zipper was easily within his range.

Carter raised his left hand and saw that his fingers were trembling. He let the hand fall back to his side. His palms were hot and wet. He raised his right hand and he didn't stop the motion to study the condition of those fingers. He grabbed the zipper and gave it a fast, violent downward pull.

Reba moaned and whirled, flinging her luscious body against him. Their searching mouths came eagerly together and her vibrant red lips were even more sweet and yielding than he'd remembered.

"I want you," she moaned.

"I want you."

His arms tightened around her and again their lips clashed, this time parting so that his insistent tongue could drive deeply into the fragrant warmth of her mouth, shocking their bodies into renewed frenzies of passion.

"God, I do want you, Reba," he growled, his fingers pulling the loosened suit down from her gorgeous white shoulders and tugging it down her body until it puddled at her feet.

She kicked the suit aside and lay across the bed. Her arms lifted, opened, inviting him to her.

Carter slid in beside her. Her lips, parted in anticipation, and her perfect white teeth drew his head down to her. At contact, her lips parted farther. She drew his tongue into her hot mouth and caressed it with her own. He felt her leg entwine around his. She wriggled herself backward on the bed until his hardness was against the warm moistness of her crevice.

She took his hand and guided it to her breast until his fingers felt the solid erectness of her large nipple.

He started to speak, but her fingers came over his lips.

"There's an old saying," she whispered. "A man talks before, a woman after. Let me do the talking."

Carter shut up and went to work.

The scent of saltwater and fish touched his nostrils as Carter dropped into the cockpit of the boat.

Bazri was waiting. The little Moroccan was at the helm. At the nod from Bazri, the engine fired up and they swung away from the pier.

Bazri came back and sat by Carter in the stern of the boat. He opened a waterproof aluminum case.

"Single-shot sniper's rifle. Ten rounds, hollow-tipped. Smoke bombs and incendiary grenades. Don't use those unless you have to. Got it?"

Carter nodded.

Bazri held up two aluminum rods and bent them into a string bow. "This will get you from the office building to the hotel roof."

"Got it. Do I swim in from the launch?"

"He'll take you in with a dinghy. It should be no

problem, but just in case, here are papers. Your driver's name is Asram. That is, if you get to the alley behind the hotel after the job is done."

"I'll get there," Carter said.

"I figure you will. Also, we got word that there will be anywhere from six to seven bodyguards around Saif. Evidently, they want to keep him alive until they find out what he's got."

"Does it matter about them?" Carter asked.

"Not at all. Fact is, most of them are nameless, but they will be a pain in the ass for you. Probably be best if you concentrate on taking them out first."

Carter nodded.

Bazri lit two cigarettes and handed Carter one of them.

He fell silent as he gazed back at the launch's wake.

"There's one more thing," he said at last.

"Yeah?" Carter said, checking the action on the rifle.

"It might prod you on a bit. Leila Samir died about two hours ago."

NINETEEN

It was one hour before dawn and the streets were just coming to life for the new day. Carter, wearing a gray and white striped djellaba and a kaffiyeh, and carrying the aluminum case, strolled easily through the pushcarts and pedestrians.

Going to be hot, he thought idly as he walked by the façade of the Hotel Sahara. He turned a corner into a poor, dimly lit quarter.

The alley led to the rear of an office building one story taller than the old hotel. It was directly across the street from the Sahara.

A lockpick let him into the rear of the building. Somewhere there was a janitor who also served as a night watchman. Carter knew that the man went to sleep one hour after his shift began and awakened ten minutes before it ended.

An elevator took him to the ninth floor. At the end of a long hall, there was an unmarked door. This led to stairs that, in turn, led to the roof.

A second lockpick opened this door. Silently, he went up the stairs. The opening at the top had no door. He set the aluminum case down and lit a cigarette. Then he stepped out onto the roof and casually strolled to the edge.

A tall, dark-suited man met him halfway. "Here, what are you doing up here?"

"I come every morning to the roof," Carter said indignantly.

"Not this morning," the man declared, sliding his hand under his coat as Carter strolled past him.

The man moved fast. Carter waited until he'd almost reached him, then whirled around, crouching low, swinging one hard-muscled leg like a solid bar at his attacker's shins, chopping down with his hand as the other man fell past him. Carter kicked at once for the ulna bone, grinning in satisfaction as the man howled in pain.

A Beretta automatic fell from his hand. Carter kicked it away, hauled the man to his feet, and rammed him against the wall.

"How many on the hotel roof?" he hissed.

The other man gasped, realization gleaming through the pain in his eyes, but he said nothing.

"*How many?*" Carter growled, closing his fingers over the man's windpipe.

"Three, just three."

Carter's right hand moved in a blur of speed. He had already flexed his forearm, dropping the stiletto into his palm. He struck just under the rib cage in an upward thrust.

The man died instantly. Carter withdrew the blade, wiped it on the man's jacket, and resheathed it.

He retrieved the case and walked to the edge of the roof. He shed the djellaba. Beneath it he wore a dark suit, off-white shirt, and a nondescript tie.

On the roof of the hotel, one story below and fifty yards away, he saw a guard move along the edge of the roof behind a chest-high wall.

Carter timed him and found he made the rounds every fifteen minutes.

He got the bow out, assembled and strung it, and took a strong, slim arrow and snapped an aluminum grappling hook onto its lead end. On the other he fastened a long, coiled lightweight nylon rope. When the guard had made his pass, Carter stood up straight, aimed the arrow toward the roof of the hotel, and drew the heavy bow to its limit. When he released, the arrow with the hook on its end went winging silently through the air, trailing the rope after it and just barely made the roof of the hotel.

He waited to see if anyone had heard the noise. The guard was obviously on the far side of the roof. He pulled on the rope until it was taut, then kept pulling until the grappling hook had secured itself on the low wall of the roof.

He tied his end of the rope to an air-vent lid and slung the rifle over his shoulder.

The last thing he took from the case was a piece of steel wire with leather thongs at each end of it. Dropping the wire over the line, Carter slid his hands through the thongs until they settled on his wrists.

He rolled over the edge of the roof and took off across the narrow expanse. Seconds later he dropped to the roof of the Hotel Sahara.

In a crouch, he checked his watch and drew the Luger from his shoulder holster. He laid the long snout of the silencer in the slant of his knees, and waited.

Exactly four minutes later, the walking guard came around the corner. Carter pumped two slugs from the Luger into his heart.

He fell with only a slight scraping sound.

The hotel was designed in the shape of a horseshoe, the open side to the rear. Carter rounded the superstructure and found the second guard sitting on an air conditioner, smoking.

He cried out just as Carter put a bullet into his brain.

The Killmaster heard running feet. Quickly he moved to a corner and settled against the concrete.

A tall woman in dark slacks and blouse with a short leather vest came around the corner. She carried a sawed-off shotgun that clattered to the roof when Carter chopped her wrist.

She started to cry out, but he muffled it. He tightened a hand around her throat and cut off her wind for a moment. Then he eased up. She gasped loudly, sucking in great lungfuls of air.

"How many more of you?" he hissed.

"Go to . . ."

He clamped his hand over her mouth again, this time covering her nostrils as well. Her eyes widened and then tried to see him, her face registering disbelief at what was happening. A moment later she was kicking and hitting, her body writhing in his tight grasp, fighting for release, for air, for life.

But then, quite suddenly, the arms went limp and her body became heavy in his arms. Carter kept his hand over her face for another thirty seconds, then let her fall to the roof at his feet.

He returned to the rope over the street. He yanked, and the slipknot on the other end gave. Quickly he hauled it in and, taking the grappling hook, went to the inner side of the roof, overlooking the courtyard.

Silently he counted inward from the rear of the hotel until he located the terrace outside Rabani Saif's suite. This done, he moved to the rear until he was directly across from the sliding glass doors.

The curtains behind the glass doors were closed. The doors themselves were cracked about a foot. Air conditioning at the Sahara, like most hotels in Aqaba, was an off-and-on luxury. Mostly off.

Carter checked his watch and then the sky. The gray

of dawn was just creeping over the horizon. In another fifteen minutes, twenty at the most, the sun would begin its ascent.

The rifle was a modified Belgian FN. It was a single-shot with a half-choke silencer. There would still be sound, but it wouldn't be readily identified as a gun exploding.

Carter chambered one shell and laid out the others on the ledge beside his arm. He sighted in on the center of the glass doors. Satisfied, he set the rifle down, out of sight behind the ledge, and walked around the roof to the door that led up from the top floor.

According to Bazri's man inside the hotel, two trays of coffee had been ordered for six o'clock sharp. One tray would go to the two men in the hallway outside Saif's room. The second would go up to the three guards on the roof.

Behind the door, Carter lit a cigarette and waited.

At exactly five minutes after six, the door opened. There were two of them, dark-suited, clones to the guard that Carter had already killed. The one in the rear carried a tray.

The first one through the door only had time to glance at Carter in surprise.

The Killmaster fired twice.

One shot ripped into his stomach, causing his hands to grab his middle convulsively. The other slug caught him as he bent down, lurching forward, and tore through the top of his head. He spun and hit the roof in a crumpled heap, his jaw moving but his eyes not seeing.

The second man dropped the tray. As it clattered down the stairs, he pulled an automatic from his belt.

Carter got off the first shot. It thudded high into the man's chest and he fell backward, careening down the stairs.

The Killmaster holstered the Luger and went down the stairs himself. He dragged the man by the heels back up to the roof, and secured the door.

It was 6:20. The sun was peeking over the horizon.

Saif had ordered his breakfast for 6:30.

Carter checked the rifle again, then leaned back against the ledge to wait.

The breakfast was five minutes late. A white-jacketed waiter threw the curtains wide and opened the glass doors. He stepped back inside the room and reemerged with a tray.

Carefully, he laid out the breakfast, and disappeared.

Inside the suite, Carter could see movement. He lifted the rifle, set it squarely on the ledge, and looked through the narrow sight.

The movement was a man, dark gray pants, no shirt. Carter couldn't see the face.

One, two, three minutes went by. The sun was up full now, and the heat haze had already started to rise from the roof beneath Carter's feet.

He ran a finger over his forehead, wiping off the perspiration, and returned his hand to the rifle.

Then he was there, Rabani Saif, beside the table, a foot from the balcony rail.

Through the sight, Carter could see the smoke curl from the end of a thin cigar clamped in the man's white teeth.

Saif stretched. His eyes came up. They opened wide when they saw the rifle and the top of Carter's head.

His head was shaking from side to side and his hands came up toward Carter in a placating gesture, palms out.

The Killmaster lowered the rifle a foot, centered on Saif's chest, and fired.

The dark mat of hair on the man's chest exploded. His body reeled backward, struck the side of one of the glass doors, and staggered.

Carter already had another shell in the FN's chamber.

The second slug widened the hole in the chest cavity, and Saif tumbled forward. He fell across the table, upending it. Dishes clattered to the floor.

Carter dropped the rifle as he heard a pounding on the door of the suite.

Going down the stairs, he peeled off the thin driving gloves and discarded them.

He opened the door of the eighth floor a crack and tossed the three smoke bombs into the hall.

At the fifth floor, he walked to room 512. The door was open a crack. He rapped and walked inside.

A maid's cart was in the center of the room. Beside it stood a little mouse of a woman. She wore a short white apron over a shapeless black dress, black stockings, and flat-heeled black shoes. Her black hair was pulled back over her narrow head and gathered into a thick braid.

In her hands she held a pair of blue coveralls.

Wordlessly, Carter climbed into the coveralls and zipped them up. From the cart he took a blue skullcap and a toolbox.

He nodded at the woman.

She nodded in return, and pushed the cart into the hall with Carter at her heels.

Two dark-suited men, their eyes wildly frantic, burst through the stairwell door. They glanced at Carter and the woman, and ran past them.

In the service elevator, the woman pushed the button for the basement. The old cage protested, but two minutes later Carter was walking toward the hotel's rear service entrance.

At the door, he discarded the toolbox and pulled the skullcap down over his forehead.

Just outside the door, there was a pushcart with a garbage can and several hard-bristled brooms.

Carter pushed the cart to the end of the alley. There were police cars converging and men running every which way.

On the street, he stopped three times to sweep papers into a pile, pick them up, and drop them into the can.

At the end of the block, parked in the mouth of an alley, was a truck with a stake bed. Straw littered the bed of the truck, and wool-heavy sheep bleated their discomfort.

The driver was a small, bald, lined, ill-shaven man with a few wisps of gray hair trailing untidily over the crown of his head and over the ear pieces of his metal-rimmed glasses.

He dropped the newspaper he was reading and nodded at Carter as the Killmaster steered the car to the rear of the truck.

By the time Carter had crawled in among the sheep, the old truck had coughed to life. He moved forward and leaned his back against the rear of the cab.

There was no window in the rear of the cab. The old man handed Carter a beat-up straw hat.

"You have had a good morning?"

"Very good," Carter replied, donning the hat and pulling it low over his eyes.

The truck coughed its way into the early-morning traffic and turned south.

In twelve hours Carter would be back in Eilat. But he wouldn't be there long.

He had made plans, with Reba.

With any luck, Washington wouldn't be able to find him for a month.

Why don't you just give it up, she had said, *and just marry me for my money?*

Carter smiled to himself.

Because, Reba, just around the corner there's another madman with another plan.

One of the lambs was licking his face.

DON'T MISS THE NEXT NEW
NICK CARTER SPY THRILLER

SANCTION TO SLAUGHTER

With the speed of a leopard, Carter opened the door and stood with the silenced gun covering the group. They had been speaking in French, but the room was silent now as every eye was upon him.

Savarin was at the head of the table, his dome-shaped head shining under the fluorescents above. Carter handed the gun to Jean and walked calmly to the man. He jerked him from his seat and hauled him along the side of the room and tossed him into the hall. Then he told Jean to back up slowly until she was in the hall, never letting the Luger waver.

When she was through the doorway, he tossed his second tiny bomb onto the table in front of the remaining men and slammed the door shut, holding it against the pressure of their attempted escape until he felt no more resistance.

"What did you do to them?" Jean asked.

Carter said nothing, now pointing his gun at Savarin.

"You killed them?"

"As they would have killed us," he growled. "C'mon, Jean, we've got work to do."

Savarin blubbered on the floor at their feet. He was incoherent, begging for his life. Carter hauled him to his feet. "How many guards in here?" he asked.

"Six," Savarin rasped through the spittle running from his mouth.

"That makes five left," Carter said as if to himself. "Now you are going to show us every part of this place, every nook and cranny."

"Shouldn't we get out of here?" Jean whispered. "You've broken their back and there are still four or five guards."

"I'd take you back if it were over," he explained. "But we've just met the drones, the ones that make it work. I found the real Guy Lafontaine a prisoner in another of their safe houses. So we have an imposter running loose. He could be the brains or he could be a pawn. We still don't know."

"I'd still like to get out of here."

"Hang in there, Jean. Something tells me we've just struck gold here. We've got to check it out."

She pulled herself together. "All right. Let's get it over with."

"How are you with weapons?"

"I've had all the courses."

"Good. First we go after the guard's automatic rifle, then we go fishing," Carter said, leading the way down the stairs, pushing the terrified man in front of him as a shield.

Jean picked up the Kalashnikov from the floor of the hall and wiped it clean. She flipped off the safety, chambered a round, and followed Carter down the stairs. "Never mind the other rifle. This one will do."

Carter smiled over his shoulder and led her to the cellar room where he'd found her. A guard was bending over his fallen comrade. Savarin called out. The man turned to be met by a 9mm bullet from Carter's Luger, and went down across the bed.

Jean took the two AK-47s they had been armed with

and emptied them. She went through the guards' pockets and came up with a well-used Makarov pistol. She slung an AK over her shoulder and held the Makarov at her side confidently. "Lead on, Commander," she said. "Let's see what this menagerie has to offer."

"What are we going to find here?" Carter asked Savarin.

The man was beyond coherent speech. His eyes had glazed over and his breathing was rapid and shallow. Carter pulled out the orange syringe and put Savarin out for the count.

"Looks like it's just you and me, pal," Jean said.

Carter could see that Jean was scared out of her mind; which was entirely natural for someone not accustomed to work in the field. He admired her bravery and would tell her so after they got out of this.

Carter found an earthen stairway to an underground cavern. It was narrow and steep, shored up with old timbers.

"Watch your step," he cautioned her.

While Carter had his attention on the uneven stairs, a guard appeared at the bottom. A shot filled the small area with sound. The Makarov barked near his ear and the guard went down.

"I owe you one," Carter said as he raced for the bottom.

"Call it even," she said, out of breath.

"No surprises now. We've got two or three other guards down here and they know they have company," he said, crouching behind a crate.

One man came running and Carter got him through the head with one shot from Wilhelmina. A second shot rang out and Jean shrieked at his side.

Carter looked around but couldn't see where the shot came from. He swung heavy crates around them and pulled the woman near him to examine her wound.

At first he couldn't see it and he'd thought he'd looked everywhere.

She groaned.

"Where are you hit?" he asked, his tone urgent. They were still in great danger.

"None of your damned business," she said, wincing.

He turned her over. The slug had creased her along the cheek of her rump. It had shocked her but she'd be all right.

"Brother Schmidt will have included some surgical dressings in the pack." He took the rucksack from his shoulders and produced a sterile dressing complete with antibiotic salve. "Put this on while I look for who shot you."

Carter crawled from behind the crates and searched the lodge from top to bottom without finding anyone.

"Any luck?" Jean asked when he returned, looking a hundred percent better.

"No. Let's look over this place together. They've got to be hiding something here," he suggested.

They began with the cavern, exploring in the dim light of a few naked bulbs.

"Look at this," Jean said after they'd been searching for a few minutes.

"Money," Carter said. "A printing press. There's got to be billions of phony dollars in this pile. What the hell for?"

"Maybe to flood the market? Topple the currency standard of the country?" she offered.

"Bizarre but possible. Let's see what the hell they've got here besides funny money."

In one corner of the huge cavern Carter found a mountain of publicity designed to foment separation and revolution. "Come look at this over here," he called to Jean.

"Soviet propaganda. Mountains of it. They've already got their propaganda machine at work."

"This will make Cuba and Nicaragua look like child's play," Jean said, scanning some of the literature. "Come look at this chart on this wall."

"My God!" Carter breathed. "It's a plan to ring the United States with missile bases just hundreds of miles from the border."

"But you'll never be able to show your little find to anyone," a voice from the top of the stairs said. "Goodbye, Commander Carlson, and you, too, Commander Sprague. It was a pleasure."

The figure of Lafontaine's double stood at the top of the stairs. Carter reached for Wilhelmina, but the man suddenly disappeared and a bundle of dynamite sat at the top of the stairs, its fuse aglow.

Carter pulled Jean behind a pile of printed matter as the blast shook the cavern. They were thrown backward against a mountain of counterfeit money as the lights went out.

They were separated.

Dust was everywhere.

The explosion had buried them alive.

—From SANCTION TO SLAUGHTER
A New Nick Carter Spy Thriller
From Jove in June 1989

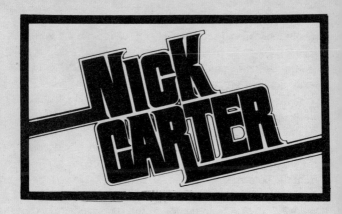

☐ 0-515-09480-0	BLOODTRAIL TO MECCA	$2.75
☐ 0-515-09519-2	DEATHSTRIKE	$2.75
☐ 0-515-09547-3	LETHAL PREY	$2.75
☐ 0-515-09584-2	SPYKILLER	$2.95
☐ 0-515-09646-8	BOLIVIAN HEAT	$2.95
☐ 0-515-09581-4	THE RANGOON MAN	$2.95
☐ 0-515-09706-3	CODE NAME COBRA	$2.95
☐ 0-515-09006-X	COUNTDOWN TO ARMAGEDDON	$2.95
☐ 0-515-09846-9	BLACK SEA BLOODBATH	$2.95
☐ 0-515-09874-4	THE DEADLY DIVA	$2.95
☐ 0-515-09923-6	INVITATION TO DEATH	$2.95
☐ 0-515-09958-9	DAY OF THE ASSASSIN	$2.95
☐ 0-515-09983-X	THE KOREAN KILL	$2.95
☐ 0-515-10014-5	MIDDLE EAST MASSACRE	$2.95
☐ 0-515-10034-X	SANCTION TO SLAUGHTER	$2.95
☐ 0-515-10060-9	HOLIDAY IN HELL	$2.95

Please send the titles I've checked above. Mail orders to:

BERKLEY PUBLISHING GROUP
390 Murray Hill Pkwy., Dept. B
East Rutherford, NJ 07073

NAME_____

ADDRESS_____

CITY_____

STATE_____ZIP_____

Please allow 6 weeks for delivery.
Prices are subject to change without notice.

POSTAGE & HANDLING:
$1.00 for one book, $.25 for each
additional. Do not exceed $3.50.

BOOK TOTAL	$_____
SHIPPING & HANDLING	$_____
APPLICABLE SALES TAX (CA, NJ, NY, PA)	$_____
TOTAL AMOUNT DUE	$_____

PAYABLE IN US FUNDS.
(No cash orders accepted.)

112